PECK'S BAD BOY
WITH THE COWBOYS

MORE WILDSIDE CLASSICS

PECK'S BAD BOY WITH THE COWBOYS

BY HON. GEO. W. PECK.

Relating the Amusing Experiences and Laughable Incidents of this Strenuous American Boy and his Pa while among the Cowboys and Indians in the Far West. Exciting Hunts and Adventures mingled with Humorous Situations and Laugh Provoking Events.

WILDSIDE PRESS

PECK'S BAD BOY WITH THE COWBOYS

This edition published 2005 by Wildside Press, LLC.
www.wildsidepress.com

CHAPTER I.

The Bad Boy and His Pa Go West — Pa Plans to Be a Dead Ringer for Buffalo Bill — They Visit an Indian Reservation and Pa Has an Encounter with a Grizzly Bear.

Well, I never saw such a change in a man as there has been in pa, since the circus managers gave him a commission to go out west and hire an entire outfit for a wild west show, regardless of cost, to be a part of our show next year. He acts like he was a duke, searching for a rich wife. No country politician that never had been out of his own county, appointed minister to England, could put on more style than Pa does.

The first day after the show left us at St. Louis we felt pretty bum, 'cause we missed the smell of the canvas, and the sawdust, and the animals, and the indescribable odor that goes with a circus. We missed the performers, the band, the surging crowds around the ticket wagon, and the cheers from the seats. It almost seemed as though there had been a funeral in the family, and we were sitting around in the cold parlor waiting for the lawyers to read the will. But in a couple of days Pa got busy, and he hired a young Indian who was a graduate of Carlisle, as an interpreter, and a reformed cowboy, to go with us to the cattle ranges, and an old big game hunter who was to accompany us to the places where we could find buffalo and grizzly bears. Pa chartered a car to take us west, and after the Indian and the cowboy and the hunter got sobered up, on the train, and got the St. Louis ptomaine poison out of their systems, and we were going through Kansas, Pa got us all into the smoking compartment.

"Gentlemen," he said, "I want you to know that this expedition is backed by the wealth of the circus world, and that there is nothing cheap about it. We are to hire, regardless of expense, the best riders, the best cattle ropers, and the best everything that goes with a wild west show. We all know that Buffalo Bill must soon, in the nature of things, pass away as a feature for shows, and I have been selected to take the place of Bill in the circus world, when he cashes in. You may have noticed that I have been letting my hair and mustache and chin whiskers grow the last few months, so that next year I will be a dead ringer for Bill. All I want is some experience as a hero of the plains, as a scout, a hunter, a scalper of Indians, a rider of wild horses, and a few things like that, and next year you will see me ride a white horse up in front of the press seats in our show, take off my broad-brimmed hat, and wave it at the crowned heads in the boxes, give the spurs to my horse, and ride away like a cavalier, and the show will go on, to the music of hand-clapping from the assembled thousands, see?"

The cowboy looked at pa's stomach, and said: "Well, Mr. Man, if you are going to blow yourself for a second Buffalo Bill, I am with you, at the salary agreed upon, till the cows come home, but you have got to show me that you have got no yellow streak, when it comes to cutting out steers that are wild and carry long horns, and you've got to rope 'em, and tie 'em all alone, and hold up your hands for judgment, in ten seconds."

Pa said he could learn to do it in a week, but the cowman said: "Not on your life." The hunter said he would be ready to call pa B. Bill when he could stand up straight, with the paws of a full-grown grizzly on each of his shoulders, and its face in front of pa's, if Pa had the nerve to pull a knife and disembowel the bear, and skin him without help. Pa said that would be right into his hand, 'cause he use to work in a slaughter house when he was a boy, and he had waded in gore.

The Indian said he would be ready to salute Pa as Buffalo Bill the Second, when Pa had an Indian's left hand tangled in his hair, and a knife in his right hand ready to scalp him, if Pa would look the Indian in the eye and hypnotize the red man so he would drop the hair and the knife, turn his back on pa, and invite him to his wigwam as a guest. Pa said all he asked was a chance to look into the very soul of the worst Indian that ever stole a horse, and he would make Mr. Indian penuk, and beg for mercy.

And we all agreed that Pa was a wonder, and then they got out a pack of cards and played draw poker awhile. Pa had bad luck, and when the Indian bet a lot of chips, Pa began to look the Indian in the eye, and the Indian began to quail, and Pa put up all the chips he had, to bluff the Indian, but Pa took his eye off the Indian a minute too quick, and the Indian quit quailing, and bet Pa $70, and Pa called him, and the Indian had four deuces and pa had a full hand, and the Indian took the money. Pa said that comes of educating these confounded red devils, at the expense of the government, and then we all went to bed.

The next morning we were at the station in the far west. We got off and started for the Indian reservation where the Carlisle Indian originally came from, and where we were to hire Indians for our show. We rode about 40 miles in hired buckboards, and just as the sun was Setting there appeared in the distance an Indian camp, where smoke ascended from tepees, tents and bark houses. When the civilized Carlisle Indian jumped up on the front seat of the buckboard and gave a series of yells that caused pa's bald head to look ashamed that it had no hair to stand on end, there came a war whoop from the camp, Indians, squaws, dogs, and everything that contained a noise letting out yells that made me sick. The Carlisle Indian began to pull off his citizen clothes of civilization, and when the horses ran down to the camp in front of the chief's tent the tribes welcomed the Carlisle prodigal son, who had removed every evidence of civilization, except a pair of football pants, and thus he reinstated himself with the affections of his race, who hugged him for joy.

Pa and the rest of us sat in the buckboard while the Indians began to feast on something cooking in a shack. We looked at each other for awhile, not daring to make a noise for fear it would offend the Indians. Pretty soon an old chief came and called Pa the Great Father, and called me a pup, and he invited us to come into camp and partake of the feast.

Well, we were hungry, and the meat certainly tasted good, and the Carlisle civilized Indian had no business to say it was dog, 'cause no man likes to smoke his pipe of peace with strong tobacco in a strange pipe, and feel that his stomach is full of dog meat. But we didn't die, and all the evening the Indians talked about the brave great father.

It seemed that they were not going to take much stock in pa's bravery until they had tried him out in Indian fashion. We were standing in the moonlight surrounded by Indians, and Pa had been questioned as to his bravery, and Pa said he was brave like Roosevelt, and he swelled out his chest and looked the part, when the chief said, pointing to a savage, snarling dog that was smelling of pa: "Brave man, kick a dog!"

We all told Pa that the Indian wanted Pa to give an exhibition of his bravery by kicking the dog, and while I could see that Pa had rather hire a man to kick the dog, he knew that it was up to him to show his mettle, so he hauled off and gave the dog a kick near the tail, which seemed to telescope the dog's spine together, and the dog landed far away. The chief patted Pa on the shoulder and said: "Great Father, bully good hero. Tomorrow he kill a grizzly," and then they let us go to bed, after Pa had explained that if everything went well he would hire all the chiefs and young braves for his show.

After we got to bed Pa said he was almost sorry he told the chief that he would take a grizzly bear by one ear, and cuff the other ear with the flat of his hand, as he didn't know but a wild grizzly would look upon such conduct differently from our old bear in the show used to. Any person around the show could slap his face, or cuff him, or kick him in the slats, and he would act as though they were doing him a favor. The big game hunter told pa that there was no danger in hunting a grizzly, as you could scare him away, if you didn't want to have any truck with him, by waving your hat and yelling: "Git, Ephraim." He said no grizzly would stand around a minute if you yelled at him. Pa made up his mind he would yell all right enough, if we came up to a grizzly.

Well, we didn't sleep much that night, 'cause Pa kept practicing on his yell to scare a grizzly, for fear he would forget the words, and when they called us in the morning Pa was the poorest imitation of a man going out to test his bravery that I ever saw. While the Indians were getting ready to go out to a canyon and turn the dogs loose to round up a bear, Pa got a big knife and was sharpening it, so he could rip the bear from Genesis to Revelations.

After breakfast the chief and the Carlisle Indian, and the big game hunter, and the cowman and I went out about two miles, to the mouth of the canyon, where it was very narrow, and they stationed Pa by a big rock, right where the bear would have to pass; the rest of us got up on a bench of the canyon, where we could see Pa be brave, and the young Indians went up about a mile, and started the dogs. Well, Pa was a sight, as he stood there waiting for the bear, so he could cuff its ears, and rip it open, right in sight of the chief, and skin it; but he was nervous, and we could see that his legs trembled when he heard the dogs bark up the canyon. I yelled to Pa to think of Teddy Roosevelt, and Daniel Boone, and Buffalo Bill, and set his teeth so they would not chatter and scare the bear, but Pa yelled back: "Never you mind, I will kill my bear in my own way, but you can make up your mind to have bear meat for supper."

Pretty soon the big game hunter said: "There he comes, sure's you are born," and we looked up the canyon, and there was something coming, as big as a load of hay, with bristles sticking up a foot high on its back, and its mouth was open, and it was loping right towards pa. Gee, but I was proud of pa, to see him sharpening his knife on his boot leg, but when the great animal got within about a block of pa, the great father seemed to have a streak of yellow, for he dropped his knife and yelled: "Git, Ephraim," in a loud voice, but Ephraim came right along, and didn't git with any great suddenness. When the bear got within about four doors of Pa, he saw the great father, and stood up on his hind legs, and looked as big as a brewery horse, and he opened his mouth and said: "Woof," just like that. That was too much for my Pa, who began to shuck his clothes, and then started on a run towards the mouth of the canyon. The bear looked around as much as to say: "Well, what do you think of that?" and we watched Pa sprinting toward the Indian camp like a scared wolf.

The big game hunter put a few bullets in the bear where they would do the most good, and killed it, and we went down in the canyon and skinned it, and took the meat and hide to camp, where we found Pa under a bed in a squaw's tepee, making grand hailing signs of distress, and trying to tell them about his killing a bear by letting it run after him, so it would tire itself out and die of heart failure.

When we found Pa he had come out from under the bed, and was looking at the hide of the bear to find the place where he hit it with the knife, as he said he could see that the only chance for him to kill the bear was to throw the knife at it from a distance, 'cause the bear was four times as big as any bear he had ever killed. Pa took out a handful of gold pieces and distributed them among the Indians, and told the Carlisle Indian to explain to the tribe that the great father had killed the bear by hypnotism, and they all believed it except the chief, who seemed skeptical, for he said: "Great father heap brave man like a sheep. Go play seven-up with squaws." Poor Pa wasn't allowed to talk with the men all day, 'cause the old chief said he was a squaw man. Pa says they don't seem to realize that a man can be brave unless he allows himself to be killed by a bear, but he says he will show them that a great mind and a great head is better in the end than foolishness. Now they want Pa to run a footrace with the young Indians, as the record he made getting to camp ahead of the bear is better than any time ever made on the reservation.

CHAPTER II.

Indian Chief Compels Bad Boy's Pa to Herd with the Squaws — He Shows Them How to Make Buckwheat Cakes and Is Kept Making Them a Week — He Talks to the Squaws About Women's Rights and They Organize a Strike — Pa's Success in a Wolf Hunt — The Strike is Put Down and the Indians Prepare to Burn Pa at the Stake.

Since Pa's experience in trying to kill a grizzly by making the animal chase him and die of heart disease, the chief has made Pa herd with the squaws, until he can prove that he is a brave man by some daring deed. The Indians wouldn't speak to him for a long time, so he decided to teach the squaws how to keep house in a civilized manner, and he began by trying to show them how to make buckwheat pancakes, so they could furnish something for the Indians to eat that does not have to be dug out of a tin can, which they draw from the Indian agent. Pa found a sack of buckwheat flour and some baking powder, and mixed up some batter, and while he was fixing a piece of tin roof for a griddle, the squaws drank the pancake batter raw, and it made them all sick, and the chief was going to have Pa burned at the stake, when the Carlisle Indian who had eaten pancakes at college when he was training with the football team, told the chief to let up on Pa and he would give them something to eat that was good, so Pa mixed some more batter and when the buckwheat pancakes began to bake, and the odor spread around among the Indians, they all gathered around, and the way they ate pancakes would paralyze you. They got some axle grease to spread on the pancakes, and fought with each other to get the pancakes, and they kept Pa baking pancakes all day and nearly all night, and then the squaws began to feel better, and Pa had to bake pancakes for them, and when the flour gave out the chief sent to the agency for more, and for a week pa did nothing but make pancakes, but finally the whole tribe got sick, and Pa had to prescribe raw beef for them, and they began to get better, and then they wanted Pa to go on a coyote hunt, and kill a kiota, which is a wolf, by jumping off his horse and taking the wolf by the neck and choking it to death. Pa said he killed a tom cat that way once, and he could kill any wolf that ever walked, so they arranged the hunt Before we went on the hunt pa sent to Cheyenne for two dozen little folding baby trundlers for the squaws to wheel the papooses in, 'cause he didn't like to see them tie the children on their backs and carry them around. Where the trundlers came Pa showed the squaws how they worked, by putting a papoose in one of the baby wagons, and pushing it around the camp, and by gosh, if they didn't make Pa wheel all the babies in the tribe, for two days, and the Indians turned out and gave the great father three cheers, but when the squaws wanted to get in the wagons and be wheeled around, Pa kicked. After teaching the squaws how to put the children in the wagons and work them, we went off on the hunt, and when we came back every squaw had her papoose in a baby wagon, but instead of wheeling the wagon in civilised fashion, they slung the wagons, babies and all, on their backs, and carried the whole thing on their backs. Gee, but that made Pa hot. He says you can't do anything with a race of people that haven't got brain enough to imitate. He says monkeys would know better than to carry baby wagons on their backs. I never thought that Indians could be jealous, but they are terrors when the jealousy germ begins to work. There is no doubt but that the squaws got to thinking a great deal of pa, 'cause he talked with them, through the Carlisle Indian for an interpreter, and as he sat on a camp chair and looked like a great white god with a red nose, and they gathered around him, and he told them stories of women in the east, and how they dressed and went to parties, and how the men worked for them that they might live in luxury, and how they had servants to do their cooking, and maids to dress them, and carriages to ride in, and lovers to slave for them, it is not to be wondered at that those poor creatures, who never had a kind word from their masters, and who were looked upon as lower than the dogs, should look upon Pa as the grandest man that ever lived, and I noticed, myself, that they gave him glances of love and admiration, and when they would snuggle up closer to pa, he would put his hand on their heads and pat their hair, and look into their big black eyes sort of tender, and pinch their brown cheeks, and chuck them under the chin, and tell them that the great father loved them, and that he hoped the time would come when every good Indian would look upon his squaw, the mother of his children, as the greatest boon that could be given to man, and that the now despised squaw would be placed on a pedestal and honored by all, and worshiped as she ought to be.

That was all right enough, but Pa never ought to have gone so far as to advise them to strike for their rights, and refuse to be longer looked upon as beasts of burden, but demand recognition as equals, and refuse longer to be drudges. I could see that trouble was brewing, for every squaw insisted on kissing the great father, and then there came a baneful light in their eyes, and they drew away together and began to talk excitedly, and Pa said he guessed they were organizing a woman's rights union. Pa and the Carlisle Indian and I went out for a stroll in the forest, and were gone an hour or so, and Pa got tired and he and I went back to camp before the Carlisle Indian did, and when we got in sight of camp we could see by the commotion that the squaw strike was on, 'cause the squaws were talking loud and the Indians were getting their guns and it looked like war. We crawled up close, and the squaws drew butcher knives and made a rush on the Indians, and the Indians weakened, and the squaws tied their hands and feet, and then the squaws had a war dance, and they told the Indians that they were now the bosses, and would hereafter run the affairs of the tribe, like white women did, and that the Indians must do the cooking, and do the work, while the squaws sat in the tents to be waited on, and that they would never do another stroke of hard work that an Indian could do. I never saw such a lot of scared Indians in my life, but when the squaws put the butcher knives to their necks, and looked fierce, and grabbed the Indians by the hair and looked as though they were going to scalp them, the Indians agreed to do all the work, and just then Pa and I came up, and the squaws hailed Pa as their deliverer, and they fell on his neck and hugged him, and they placed a camp chair for him, and put a tiger skin cloak around him, and a necklace of elk's teeth around his neck, and all kneeled down and seemed to be worshiping him, while the Indians looked on in the most hopeless manner, and then the Carlisle Indian came and said the squaws had made Pa the chief squaw of the tribe, and that the Indians had agreed to do the work hereafter. Pa counted the elk teeth on his necklace and figured that he could sell them for two dollars apiece, and pay the expenses of the trip. Then the squaws cut the strings that bound the Indians, and set them to work cooking dinner, and it was awful the way the spirit seemed to be knocked out of the Indians, just by a little rising on the part of the downtrodden squaws. The Indians cooked dinner, and waited on the squaws, and Pa and all of us whites, and after dinner the squaws ordered the horses and the squaws and us whites went off on a wolf hunt, with the dogs, where Pa was to show his bravery to the squaws instead of the Indians. The squaws gave Pa the old chief's horse, and the best one in the tribe, and leaving the chief to wash the dishes, and the Indians to clean up the camp, and clean some fish for supper, the victorious squaws with Pa at the head, and the rest of us whites on ponies, went out on the mesa and turned the dogs loose, and pretty soon they were after a wolf and Pa led out ahead on his racing pony, cheered by the yells of the squaws, and it was a fine race for about two miles. Pa and the cowboy and the big game hunter and I got ahead of the squaws, and after awhile we got up pretty near to the wolf, and the big game hunter said to pa: "Now, old man, is your chance to make yourself solid with the squaws. We will hold hack and when the dogs get the wolf surrounded you rush in and kill him or your name's Dennis." Pa said: "You watch my smoke, and see me eat that wolf alive." So we held up our horses, and let Pa go ahead. He rode up to the wolf, and I never saw a man with such luck as Pa had. Just as he got near the wolf and the animal showed his teeth, Pa tried to steer his horse away from the savage animal, but the horse stumbled in a prairie dog hole, and fell right on top of the wolf, crushing the life out of the animal, and throwing Pa over his head. Pa was stunned, but he soon came to, and when he realized that the wolf was dead, he grabbed the animal by the neck with one hand, and by the lower jaw with the other, and held on to it till the crowd came up, and when the squaws saw that Pa had killed the biggest wolf ever seen on the reservation, by rushing in single handed and choking the savage animal to death, they gave Pa an ovation that was enough to turn the head of any man. Us white fellows knew that Pa couldn't have been hired to go near that wolf until the horse fell on it and killed it, but we wanted to give Pa a reputation for bravery, and so we let the squaws compliment Pa and hug him, and make him think he was a holy terror. So they tied the wolf on the saddle in front of pa, and we all went back to camp, the squaws shouting for pa, and telling the Indians how the great white father had strangled the father of all wolves, and then the Indians served the fish supper, and all looked as though there had been a bloodless revolution, and that the squaws were in charge of the government, and Pa was "it," but I could see the Carlisle Indian whispering to the Indians, and it seemed to me I could see signs of an uprising, and when the Indians had the supper dishes washed, and all seemed going right, and the squaws were rejoicing at being emancipated, just as the sun was setting, every Indian pulled out a bull whip and began to lash the squaws to their tents, and some young braves grabbed Pa and removed the leopard skin cloak, and the elk's teeth necklace, and tied his hands and feet, and carried him into a circle made by the Indians. I asked the Carlisle Indian what was the matter, and he said, pointing to some wood that had been piled at the roots of a tree: "The great white father is going to be tried for inciting a rebellion among the squaws, and the chances are that before the sun shall rise tomorrow your old dad will be broiled, fricasseed and baked to a turn." I went up to Pa and said: "Gee, dad, but they are going to burn you at the stake," and Pa called the cowboy, and told him to ride to the military post and ask for a detail of soldiers to hurry up and put a stop to it, and then Pa said to me: "Hennery, it may look as though I was in a tight place, but I place my trust in the squaws and soldiers," and Pa rolled over to take a nap.

CHAPTER III.

How the Old Man Subdued the Indians with an Electric Battery and Phosphorus — He Tries His Hand at Roping a Steer — The Disastrous Result.

Gee, but I thought Pa was all in when I closed by last letter, when the Indians had him bound on a board, and had lighted a fire, and were just going to broil him. Jealousy is bad enough in a white man, but when an Indian gets jealous of his squaw there is going to be something doing, and when a whole tribe gets jealous of one old man, 'cause he has taught the squaws to be independent, and rise up as one man against the tyranny of their husbands, that white man is not safe, and as Pa lay there, waiting for the fire to get hot enough for them to lay him on the coals, I felt almost like crying, 'cause I didn't want to take pa's remains back home so scorched that they wouldn't be an ornament to society, so I went up to pa's couch to get his instructions as to our future course, when he should be all in.

I said, "Pa, this is the most serious case you have yet mixed up in. O, wimmen, how you do ruin men who put their trust in you."

Pa winked at me, and said:

"Never you mind me, Hennery. I will come out of this scrape and have all the Indians on their kpeesan less than an hour, begging my pardon," and then Pa whispered to me, and I went to pa's valise and got an electric battery and put it in pa's pocket and scattered copper wires all around pa's body, and fixed it so pa could touch a button and turn on a charge of electricity that would paralyze an elephant, and then I got some matches and took the phosphorus off and put it all over pa's face and hands and clothes and as it became dark and the phosphorus began to shine, Pa was a sight. He looked like moonlight on the lake, and I got the cowboy and the big game hunter and the educated Indian to get down on their knees around pa, and chant something that would sound terrible to the Indians. The only thing in the way of a chant that all of them could chant was the football tune, "There'll Be a Hot Time in the

Old Town Tonight," and we were whooping it up over pa's illuminated remains when the Indians came out to put Pa on the fire, and when they saw the phosphorescent glow all over him, and, his face looking as though he was at peace with all the world, and us whites on our knees, making motions and singing that hot dirge, they all turned pale, and were scared, and they fell back reverently, and gazed fixedly at poor pa, who was winking at us, and whispering to us to keep it up, and we did.

The old chief was the first to recover, and he saw that something had to be done pretty quick, so he talked Indian to some of the braves, and I slipped away and put some phosphorus all over a squaw, and she looked like a lightning bug, and told her to go and fall on pa's remains and yell murder. The Indians had started to grab Pa and put him on the fire when Pa turned on the battery and the big chief got a dose big enough for a whole flock of Indians, and all who touched Pa got a shock, and they all fell back and got on their knees, and just then the squaw with the phosphorus on her system came running out, and she fell across pa's remains, and she shone so you could read fine print by the light she gave, and that settled it with the tribe, 'cause they all laid down flat and were at pa's mercy. Pa pushed the illuminated squaw away, and went around and put his foot on the neck of each Indian, in token of his absolute mastery over them, and then he bade them arise, and he told them he had only done these things to show them the power of the great father over his children, and now he would reveal to them his object in coming amongst them, and that was to engage 20 of the best Indians, and 20 of the best squaws, to join our great show, at an enormous salary, and be ready in two weeks to take the road. The Indians were delighted, and began to quarrel about who should go with the show, and to quiet them Pa said he wanted to shake hands with all of them, and they lined up, and Pa took the strongest wire attached to the battery in his pistol pocket, and let it run up under his coat and down his sleeve, into his right hand, and that was the way he shook hands with them. I thought I would die laughing. Pa took a position like a president at a New Year's reception, and shook hands with the tribe one at a time. The old chief came first, and Pa grasped his hand tight, and the chief stood on his toes and his knees knocked together, his teeth chattered, and he danced a cancan while Pa held on to his hand and squeezed, but he finally let go and the chief wiped his hand on a dog, and the dog got some of the electricity and ki yield to beat the band. Then Pa shook hands with everybody, and they all went through the same kind of performance, and were scared silly at the supernatural power Pa seemed to have. The squaws seemed to get more electricity than the buck Indians, 'cause Pa squeezed harder, and the way they danced and cut up didoes would make you think they had been drinking. Finally Pa touched them all with his magic wand, and then they prepared a feast and celebrated their engagement to go with the circus, and we packed up and got ready to go to a cattle round up the next day at a ranch outside the Indian reservation, where Pa was to engage some cowboys for the show. As we left the headquarters on the reservation the next morning all the Indians went with us for a few miles, cheering us, and Pa waved his hands to them, and said, "bless you, me children," and looked so wise, and so good, and great that I was proud of him. The squaws threw kisses at pa, and when we had left them, and had got out of sight, Pa said, "Those Indians will give the squaws a walloping when they get back to camp, but who can blame them for falling in love with the great father?" and then pa winked, and put spurs to his pony and we rode across the mesa, looking for other worlds to conquer.

On the way to the ranch where we were to meet the cowboys and engage enough to make the show a success, the cowboy Pa had along told Pa that it might be easy enough to fool Indians with the great father dodge, and the electric battery, and all that, but when he struck a mess of cowboys he would find a different proposition, 'cause he couldn't fool cowboys a little bit. He said if Pa was going to hire cowboys, he had got to be a cowboy himself, and if he couldn't rope steers he would have to learn, 'cause cowboys, if they were to be led in the show by pa, would want him to be prepared to rope anything that had four feet. Pa said while he didn't claim to be an expert, he had done some roping, and could throw a lasso, and while he didn't always catch them by the feet, when he tried to, he got the rope over them somewhere, and if the horse he rode knew its business he ultimately got his steer, and he would be willing to show the boys what he could do.

We got to the cow camp in time for dinner, and our cowboy introduced Pa to the cowboys around the chuck wagon, and told them Pa was an old cowboy who had traveled the Texas trail years ago, and was one of the best horsemen in the business, a manager of a show that was adding a wild west department and wanted to hire 40 or more of the best ropers and riders, at large salaries, to join the show, and that Pa considered himself the legitimate successor of Buffalo Bill, and money was no object. Well, the boys were tickled to meet pa, and some said they had heard of him when he was roping cattle on the frontier, and that tickled pa, and they smoked cigarettes, and finally saddled up and began to brand calves and rope cattle to get them where they belonged, each different brand of cattle being driven off in a different direction, and we had the most interesting free show of bucking horses and roping cattle I ever saw. Pa watched the boys work for a long time, and complimented them, or criticised them for some error, until the crazy spirit seemed to get into him, and he thought he could do it as well as any of the boys, and he told our cowboy that whenever the boys got tired he would like to get on a buckskin pony that one of the men was riding, and show that while a little out of practice he could stand a steer on its head, and get off his horse and tie the animal in a few seconds beyond the record time.

I told Pa he better hire a man to do it for him, but he said, "Hennery, here is where your Pa has got to make good, or these cowboys won't affiliate. You take my watch and roll, 'cause no one can tell where a fellow will land when he gets his steer," and I took pa's valuables and the boys brought up the buckskin horse, which smelled of Pa and snorted, and didn't seem to want Pa to get on, but they held the horse by the bridle, and Pa finally got himself on both sides of the horse, and took the lariat rope off the pommel of the saddle and began to handle it, kind of awkward, like a boy with a clothesline. I didn't like the way the cowboys winked around among themselves and guyed pa, and I told Pa about it, and tried to get him to give it up, but he said, "When I get my steer tied, and stand with my foot on his neck, these winking cowboys will take off their hats to me all right. I am Long Horn Ike, from the Brazos, and you watch my smoke."

Well, the boys tightened up the cinch on pa's saddle, and pointed out a rangy black steer in a bunch down on the flat, and told pa the game was to cut that steer out of the bunch and rope it, and tie it, and hold up his right hand for the time keeper to record it. Gee, but Pa spurred the horse and rode into that bunch of cattle like a whirlwind, and I was proud of him, and he cut out the black steer all right, and rode up near it, and swung his lariat, and sent it whizzing through the air, and the noose went out over the head and neck and fore feet of the steer, and the horse stopped and set itself back on its haunches, and the rope got around the belly of the steer, and when the rope became taut, and the steer ought to have been turned bottom-side up, the cinch of pa's saddle broke, the saddle came off with pa hugging his legs around it, and the black steer started due west for Texas, galloping and bellowing, and you couldn't see Pa and the saddle for the dust they made following the steer. If Pa had let go of the saddle, he would have stopped, but he hung to it, and the rope was tied to the saddle. The buckskin horse, relieved of the saddle, looked around at the cowboys as much as to say, "wouldn't that skin you," and went to grazing, the other cattle looked on as though they would say, "Another tenderfoot gone wrong," and as the black steer and Pa and the saddle went over a hill, Pa only touching the high places, the boss cowboy said, "Come on and help head off the steer, and send a wagon to bring back the remains of Long Horn Ike from the Brazos," and then I began to cry for pa.

CHAPTER IV.

Pa, the Bad Boy and a Band of Cowboys Go in Search of a
Live Dinosaurus — The Expedition is Captured by a Gang of
Train Robbers and Pa is Held for Ransom.

When I saw Pa clinging to the saddle, which had got loose from the horse that he was riding when he lassoed the black steer around the belly, and the steer was running away, dragging Pa and the saddle across the plains, I thought I never would see him alive again. But the cowboys said they would bring his remains back all right. When they rode away to capture the steer and release pa, I stopped crying and laid down under the chuck wagon with the dogs, to think over what I would do, alone in the world, and I must have fallen asleep, for the next thing I knew the dogs barked and woke me up, and I looked off to the south and the cowboys were coming back with pa's remains on a buckboard.

I went up to the wagon to see if Pa looked natural, and he raised up, like a corpse coming to, and said: "Hennery, did you notice how I roped the black steer?" and I said: "Yes, pa, I saw the whole business, and saw you start south, chasing the steer, armed only with a saddle, and what is the news from Texas?"

Pa said: "Look-a-here, I don't want to hear any funny business. I delivered the goods all right, and if the cinch of the saddle had held out faithful to the end, I would have tied the steer in record time, but man proposes and the rest you have to leave to luck. I was out of luck, that is all, but the ride I had across the prairie has given me some ideas about flying machines that will be worked into our show next year."

Pa got up off the buckboard and shook himself, and he was just as well and hearty as ever, and the cowboys got around him, and told him he was a wonder, and that Buffalo Bill couldn't hold a candle to him as an all-around rough rider and cowboy combined. So pa hired about a dozen of the cowboys to go with our show, and then we went into camp for the night, and the cowboys told of a place about 20 miles away, where some scientists had a camp, where they were excavating to dig out petrified bone of animals supposed to be extinct, like the dinosaurus and the hoday, and Pa wanted to go there and see about it, and the next day we took half a dozen of the cowboys Pa had hired, and we rode to the camp.

Gee, but I never believed that such animals ever did exist in this country, but the scientists had one animal picture that showed the dinosaurus as he existed when alive, an animal over 70 feet long, that would weigh as much as a dozen of our largest elephants, with a neck as long as 15 giraffes, and then they showed us bones of these animals that they dug out and put together, and the completed mess of bones showed that the dinosaurus could eat out of a six-story window, and pa's circus instinct told him that if he could find such an animal alive, and capture it for the show, our fortunes would be made.

We stayed there all night, and Pa asked questions about the probability of there being such animals alive at this day, and the scientists promptly told Pa these animals only existed ages and ages ago, when the country was covered with water and was a part of the ocean, and that the animals lived on the high places, but when the water receded, and the ocean became a desert, the dinosaurus died of a broken heart, and all we had to show for it was these petrified bones.

Pa ought to have believed the scientists, 'cause they know all about their business, but after the scientists had gone to bed the cowboys began to string pa. They told him that about a hundred miles to the north, in a valley in the mountains, the dinosaurus still existed, alive, and that no man dare go there. One cowboy said he was herding a bunch of cattle in a valley up there once, and the bunch got into a drove of dinosauruses, and the first thing he knew a big dinosaurus reached out his neck and picked up a steer, raised it in the air about 80 feet, as easy as a derrick would pick up a dog house, and the dinosaurus swallowed the steer whole, and the other dinosauruses each swallowed a steer. The cowboy said before he knew it his whole bunch of steers was swallowed whole, and they would have swallowed him and his horse if he hadn't skinned out on a gallop. He said he could hear the dinosauruses for miles, making a noise like distant thunder, whether from eating the steers, giving them a pain, or whether bidding defiance to him and his horse, he never could make out but he said nothing but money could ever induce him to go into that valley again.

Pa asked the other cowboys if they had ever been to that dinosaurus valley, and they winked at each other and said they had heard of it, but there was not money enough to hire them to go there, 'cause they had heard that a man's life was not safe a minute. Bill, who had told the story, was the only man who had ever been there, and the only man living that had seen a live dinosaurus.

Then we turned in, and Pa never slept a wink all night, thinking of the rare animals, or insects, or reptiles, or whatever they are, that he expected to land for the show. He whispered to me in the night and said: "Hennery, I am on the trail of the dinosaurus, and while I am not prepared to capture one alive, at this time, I am going to that valley and see the animals alive, and make plans for their capture, and report to the management of the show. What do you think about it?"

I told Pa that I thought that cowboy, Bill, was the worst liar that we had ever run up against, and I knew by studying geography in school that the dinosaurus was extinct, and had been for thousands of years. Pa said: "So they say the buffalo is extinct, but you can find 'em, if you have got the money. Lots of thing are extinct, till some brave explorer penetrates the fastnesses and finds them. The mastodon is extinct, according to the scientists, but they are alive in Alaska. The north pole is extinct, but some dub in a balloon will find it all right. I tell you, I am going to see a live dinosaurus, or bust. You hear me?" and Pa heard them cooking breakfast, and we got up.

Before noon Pa had organized a pack train and hired three cowboys, and got some diagrams and pictures of dinosauruses from the scientists, and we started north on the biggest fool expedition that ever was, but Pa was as earnest and excited as Peary planning a north pole expedition, and as busy as a boy killing snakes. After the cowboys and the scientists had tried to get Pa to make his will before he went, and got the addresses where Pa wanted our remains sent to in case of our being found dried up on the prairie, and our bones polished by wolves, we were on the move, and Pa was so happy you would think he had already found a live dinosaurus, and had him in a cage.

For four days we rode along up and down foothills, and divides, and small mountains, and all the time Pa was telling the boys how, after we had located our dinosauruses, we would go back east and organize an expedition with derricks and cages as big as a house, and come back and drive the animals in. And when we got them with the show people we would run trains hundreds of miles to see the rarest animals any show ever exhibited to a discriminating public, and we could charge five dollars for tickets, and people would mob each other to get up to the ticket wagon. Then the boys would wink at each other, and tap their foreheads with their fingers, and look at Pa as though they expected he would break out violently insane any minute.

Finally we got up on a high ridge, and a beautiful, fertile valley was unfolded to our view, and Bill, the cowboy who had had his herd of steers eaten by the dinosaurus, said that was the place, and he began to shiver like he had the ague. He said he wouldn't go any farther without another hundred dollars, and Pa asked the other cowboys if they were afraid, too, and they said they were a little scared, but for another hundred dollars they would forget it, forget their families, and go down into the death valley.

Pa paid them the money, and we went down into the valley, and rode along, expecting to jump a flock of dinosauruses any minute, but the valley was as still as death, and Pa said to Bill: "Why don't you bring on your dinosauruses," and Bill said he guessed by the time we got up to the far end of the valley we would see something that would make us stand without hitching.

We went on towards where the valley came to a point where there seemed to be a hole in the side of the mountain, when all of a sudden four or five gun shots were heard, and four of our horses dropped dead in their tracks, and about a dozen men come out of the hole in the wall and told us to hold up our hands, and when we did so they took our guns away and told us to come in out of the wet.

We went into a cave and found that we had been captured by Curry's gang of train robbers, who made their headquarters in the hole in the wall. The leader searched Pa and took all his money, and told us to make ourselves at home. Pa protested, and said he was an old showman who had come to the valley looking for the supposed-to-be-extinct dinosaurus, to capture one for the show, and the leader of the gang said he was the only dinosaurus there was, but he hadn't been captured. Then the leader slapped our cowboys on the shoulders and told them they had done a good job to bring into camp such a rich old codger as Pa was, and then we found that the cowboys belonged to Curry's gang, and had roped Pa in in order to get a ransom.

The leader asked Pa about how much he thought his friends at the east could raise to get him out, and when Pa found he was in the hands of bandits, and that the dinosaurus mine was salted, and he had been made a fool of, he said to me: "Hennery, now, honest, between man and man, wouldn't this skin you?"

I began to cry and said: "Pa, both of us are skun. How are we going to get out of this?" and Pa said: "Watch me."

CHAPTER V.

*Pa and the Bad Boy Among the Train Robbers — Pa Tries to
Persuade the Head Bandit to Become a Financier — The
Bandit Prefers Train Robbery and Puts Up a Good Argument.*

I used to think I would like to be a train robber, and have a nice
gang of boys to do my bidding. I have often pictured my gang
putting a red light on the track and stopping a train laden with
gold, holding a revolver to the head of the engineer, and compelling him to go and dynamite the express car. Then we would fill our
pockets and haversacks with rolls of bills that would choke a hip-
popotamus, and ride away to our shack in the mountains, divide
up the swag, go on a trip to New York, bathe in champagne, dress
like millionaires, go to theaters morning, noon and night, eat lob-
ster until our stomachs would form an anti-lobster union, and be
so gay the people would think we were young Vandergoulds. Since
Pa and I were captured by the Hole-in-the-Wall gang I have found
that all is not glorious in the train-robbing and capturing-for-ran-
som business, and that robbers are never happy except when a robbery is safely over, and the gang gets good and drunk.

The first day or two after Pa and I and the traitorous cowboys
were captured, we had a pretty nice time, eating canned stuff and
elk meat, and Pa was kept busy telling the gang of what had happened in the outside world for several months, as the gang did not
read the daily papers. When they robbed a train they let the
newsboy alone for fear he would get the drop on them.

Pa told them about the wave of reform that was going over the
country, and how the politicians were taking the railroads and
monopolists by the neck, and shaking them like a terrier would
shake a rat; how the insurance companies that had been for years
tying the policy holders hand and foot, and searching their pockets
for illicit gains had been caught in the act, and how the presidents
and directory were liable to have to serve time in the penitentiary.
Pa told the Hole-in-the-Wall gang all the news until he got hoarse.

"And how is my old friend Teddy, the rough rider?" asked one of the gang, who claimed he had gone up to San Juan hill with the president.

"The president is in fine shape," said pa, "and he is making friends every day, fighting the trusts, and trying to save the people from ruin."

"Gee, but what a train robber Teddy would have made, if he had turned his talents in that direction, instead of wasting his strenuousness in politics," said the leader of the gang. "I would give a thousand dollars to see him draw a bead on the engineer of a fast mail, and make him get down and do the dynamite act, and then load up the saddle bags and pull out for the Hole-in-the-Wall. That man has wasted his opportunities, and instead of being at the head of a gang of robbers, with all the world at his feet, ready to hold up their hands at the slightest hint, living a life of freedom in the mountains, there he is doing political stunts, and wearing boiled clothes, and eating with a fork." And the bandit sighed for Teddy.

"Well, he will make himself just as famous," said pa, "if he succeeds in landing the holdup men of Wall street, and compelling them to disgorge their stealings. But say," said pa, looking the leader of the bandit gang square in the eyes, "why don't you give up this bad habit of robbing people with guns, and go back east and enter some respectable business and make your mark? You are a born financier, I can see by the way you divide up the increment when you rob a train. You would shine in the business world. Come on, go back east with me, and I will use my influence to get you in among the men who own automobiles and yachts, and drive four-in-hands. What do you say?"

"No, it is too late," said the leader of the Hole-in-the-Wall gang of train robbers, with a sigh. "I should be outclassed if I went into Wall street now. I have got many of the elements in my make up of the successful financier, and the oil octopus, and if I had not become a train robber I might have been a successful insurance president, but I have always been handicapped by a conscience. I could not rob widows and orphans if I tried. It would give me a pain that medicine would not cure to know that women and children were crying for bread because I had robbed them and was living high on their money. If it wasn't for my conscience I could take the presidency of a life insurance company, and rob right and left, equal to any of the crowned heads who are now in the business. But if I was driving in my automobile and should run over a poor woman who might be a policy holder, I could not act as would be expected of me, and look around disdainfully at her mangled body in the road, and sneer at her rapidly cooling remains, and put on steam and skip out with my mask on. I would want to choke off the snorting, bad-smelling juggernaut and get out and pick up the dear old soul and try to restore her to consciousness, which act would cause me to be boycotted by the automobile murderers' union and I would be a marked man.

"As president of a life insurance company I could not vote myself a hundred and fifty thousand dollars a year salary, and take it from fatherless children and widows and retain my self respect. Out here in the mountains I can occasionally take my boys, when our funds get low, and ride away to a railroad, and hold up the choo-choo cars, and take toll, but not of the poor passengers. Who do we rob? Why the railroads are owned by Standard Oil, and if we take a few thousand dollars, all Mr. Rockefeller has to do is to raise the price of kerosene for a day or two and he comes out even. The express car stuff is all owned by Wall street, and when we take the contents of a safe, ten thousand or twenty thousand dollars, the directors of the express company sell stock short in Wall street and make a million or so to cover the loss by the bandits of the far west, and pocket the balance. So you see we are doing them a favor to rob a train, and my conscience is clear. I am always sorry when an engineer or expressman is killed, and when such a thing occurs I find out the family and send money to take care of them, but of late years we never kill anybody, because the train hands don't resist any more, for they do not care to die to save Wall street money. Now when I say to an engineer: 'Charley, turn her off and stop here in the gulch and take a dynamite stick and go wake up the express fellow by blowing off the door of his car,' the engineer wipes his hands on his overalls and says: 'All right, Bill, but don't point that gun at my head, 'cause it makes me nervous.' He blows up the express car as a matter of accommodation to me, and the expressman comes to the door, rubbing his sleepy eyes open and says: 'It's a wonder you wouldn't let a man get a little rest. That dinky little safe in the corner hasn't got anything in it to speak of.' And then we blow up the little safe first, and maybe find all we want, and we hurry up, so the boys can go on about their business as quietly as possible. It is all reduced to a system, now, like running a railroad or pipe lines, and I am contented with my lot, and there is no strain on my conscience, as there would be if I was robbing poor instead of the rich. Of course, there are some things that I would like to have the government do, like building us a house and furnishing us steam heat, because these caves are cold and in time will make us rheumatic, but I can wait another year, when we shall send a delegate to congress from this district who will look out for our interests. The Mormons are represented in congress, and I don't see why we shouldn't be."

"Well, you have got gall, all right," said Pa to the bandit. "You mean to tell me you had rather pursue your course as a train robber, away out here in the mountains with no doctor within a hundred miles of you, and no way to spend your money after you get it, sleeping nights on the rocks and eating canned stuff you pack in here after robbing a grocery, than to enter the realms of high finance and be respected by the people, and be one of the people, with no price on your head, one of the great body of eighty million men who rule a country that is the pride of the earth? You must be daffy," said pa, just as disgusted as he could be.

"Sure, Mike," said the robber. "Everybody here respects me, and who respects the Wall street high finance and life insurance robber? Not even their valets. Me one of the people? Ye gods, but you watch these same people for a few years. You say they run the government! They and their government are run by Wall street, which owns the United States senate, body and soul. The people are pawns on a chess board, moved by the players, and they only talk, while the Wall street owners act. Let me tell you a story. I once had a dog trained so that he would lay down and roll over for a cracker, and would hold a piece of meat on his nose until his mouth would water and his eyes sparkle, but he would wait for me to snap my fingers before he would toss the meat in the air with his nose and snatch it in his mouth, and swallow it whole for fear I would get it away from him. He would stand on his hind legs and speak and beg for a bone to be thrown to him so he could catch it. Do you know, the people of this country remind me of that dog. If they do not assert themselves and take monopoly, high finance, insurance robbery, grafting and millionaire and billionaire owner-ship of everything that pays by the throat and strangle them all, and do business themselves instead of having business done for them by the money power, they will never get noticed except when they do their tricks like my old dog. When the time comes that the people wear collars and are led by chains, and they have to stand on their hind legs and speak to their rich and arrogant masters for bones, and hold meat on their noses until Wall street snaps its fin-gers, you will want to come out here in the mountains and live the free life of a train robber with a conscience. What do you think about it, bub?" said the robber to me.

"Well," says I to him, "you talk like a socialist, or a Democrat, but you talk all right. If I am one of the people I will do as the rest do, but I'll be darned if I will get down and roll over for anybody."

CHAPTER VI.

Pa Plays Surgeon and Earns the Good Will of the Bandits —
They Give Him a Course Dinner — Speeches Follow the
Banquet — Pa is Made Honorary Member of the Band — Pa
and the Bad Boy Allowed to Go Free Without Ransom.

We had the worst and the best two weeks of our lives while prisoners of the train robbers at the Hole-in-the-Wall, because we had plenty to eat, and good company, with hunting for game in the foothills by day, and cinch at night, but the sleeping on the rocks of the cave, with buffalo robes for beds, was the greatest of all. Pa got younger every day, but he yearned to be released and would look for hours down the dinosaurus valley, hoping to see soldiers or circus men who might hear of our capture, charging down the opposite hills and up the valley to our rescue, but nobody ever came, and Pa felt like Robinson Crusoe on the island.

Some times for a couple of days the robbers would go away to rob a train or a stage coach, and leave us with a few guards, who acted as though they wanted us to try to escape, so they could shoot us in the back, but we stayed, and fried bacon and elk meat and sighed for rescue.

One day the robbers came back from a raid with piles of greenbacks as big as a bale of hay, and it was evident they had robbed a train and been resisted, because one man had a bullet in his thigh, and Pa had to use his knowledge of surgery to dig out the shot, and he made a big bluff at being a surgeon, and succeeded in getting the balls out and healing up the sores, so the bandits thought Pa was great. When he insisted that the leader let him know how much it would be to ransom us, so we could send to the circus for money, the leader told Pa he had been such a decent prisoner, and had been such good company, and had been such a help in digging the bullets out of the wounded, that the gang was going to let us go free, without taking a cent from us, but was going to consider us honorary members of the gang and divide the money they had secured in the last holdup with us.

Pa said he wanted his liberty, thanked the leader for his kind words, but he said there was a strong feeling in the east against truly good people like himself taking tainted money, and while he would not want to make a comparison between the methods men adopt to secure tainted money, in business or highway robbery, he hoped the gang to which he had been elected an honorary member would not insist on his carrying away any of the tainted money.

"You are all right in theory, old man," said the leader of the gang, "but this money which might have been tainted when it was chipped by express from Wall street to the far west, has been purified by passing through our hands, where it has been carried over mountain ranges on pack horses, in blizzards, till every tainted germ has been blown away. Now, we propose to give you a banquet tomorrow night, at which we shall all make speeches, and then you will be provided with horses, supplies and money, and guided away from here blindfolded, and within 48 hours you will be free as the birds, and all we ask is that you will never give us and our hiding place away to Billy Pinkerton. Is it a go?"

Pa said it was a go all right except taking the tainted money, but he would think it over, and dream over it, and maybe take his share of the swag, but he wanted to be allowed to return it if, after calling a meeting of his board of directors, they should refuse to receive the tainted money. Pa added that the board of directors of a circus might not be as particular as a church or college, and he thought he could assure the gang that the money would not come back to bother them.

The leader of the gang said that would be all right, and for pa and I and the boys to begin to pack up and get ready to return to civilization and all its wickedness. We worked all day and played cinch for hundred dollar bills all the evening, and the next day arranged for the banquet.

When night came, and the pine knots were lit in the cave, about 15 bandits and Pa and I sat down to a course banquet on the floor of the cave, and ate and drank for an hour. We had few dishes, except tin cups and tin plates, but it was a banquet all right. The first course was soup, served in cans, each man having a can of soup with a hole in the top, made by driving a nail through the tin, and we sucked the soup through the hole. The next course was fish, each man having a can of sardines, and we ate them with hard tack. Then we had a game course, consisting of fried elk, and then a salad of canned baked beans, and coffee with condensed milk, and a spoonful or two of condensed milk for ice cream. When the banquet was over the leader of the bandits rapped on the stone floor of the cave with the butt of his revolver for attention, and taking a canteen of whisky for a loving cup, he drank to the health of their distinguished guest, and passed it around, so all might drink, and then he spoke as follows:

"Fellow Highway Robbers: We have with us tonight one who comes from the outside world, with all its wickedness, this old man, simple as a child, and yet foxy as the world goes, this easy mark who is told that the dinosaurus still exists, and believes it, and comes to this valley to find it. If some one told him that Adam and Eve were still alive, and running a stock ranch up in the Big Horn basin, he would believe it, and if it came to him as a secret that Solomon in all his glory was placer mining in a distant valley over the mountains, he would rush off to engage Solomon to drive a chariot next year in his show. Such an ability to absorb things that are not so, in a world where all men are suspicious of each other, should be encouraged. This old man comes to our quiet valley, where all is peace, and where we are honest, fresh from the wicked world, where grafting is a science respected by many, and where the bank robber who gets above a million is seldom convicted and always respected, while we, who only occasionally meet a train with a red light and pass the plate, and take up a slight collection, are looked upon as men who would commit a crime. Why, gentlemen, our profession is more respectable than that of the man who is appointed administrator of the estate of his dead friend, and who blows in the money and lets the widow and orphan go to the poorhouse, or the officer of a savings bank who borrows the money of the poor and when they hear that he is flying high demand their money, and he closes the bank, and eventually pays seven cents on the dollar, and is looked upon as a great financier. It has been a pleasure to us to have this kindly old man visit us, and by his example of the Golden Rule, to do to others as you would be done by, make us contented with our lot. We are not the kind of business men who try to ruin the business of competitors by poisoning their wells, or freezing them out of business. If any other train robbers want to do business in our territory, they have the same rights that we have, and the world is big enough for all to ply their trade. Now I am going to call upon our friend, Buckskin Bill, my associate in crime, who was wounded by a misdirected load of buckshot in our latest raid, which buckshot were so ably removed from his person by our distinguished friend who is so soon to leave us," and the leader again passed the loving cup and gave way to Buckskin Bill, who said:

"Pals — I do not know if you have ever suspected that before I joined this bunch I was steeped in crime, but I must confess to you that I was a Chicago alderman for one term, during the passage of the gas franchise and the traction deal, but I trust I have reformed, because I have led a different life all these years, I like this free life of the mountains, where what you get in a holdup is yours, and you do not have to divide with politicians, and if you refuse to divide they squeal on you, and you see the guide board pointing to Joliet. I would not go back to the wicked life of an alderman, to make a dishonest living by holding up bills until the agent came around and gave me an envelope, but I do want to hear from my old pals in the common council, and I would ask our corpulent friend, who so ably picked the buckshot out of my remains, when he passes through Chicago to go to the council chamber and give my benediction to my colleagues, and ask them to repent before it is too late, and come west and go into legitimate robbery, far away from the sleuths who are constantly on their trails. While the lamp continues to burn the vilest alderman may buy a ticket to the free and healthy west, and we will give him a welcome. Old man, shake," and Buckskin Bill shook pa's hand and sat down on his knees, because his wounds were not healed.

The leader of the gang then called upon Pa for a few remarks, and Pa said: "Gentlemen, you have done me great honor to make me an honorary member of your organization, and I shall go away from here with a feeling that you are the highest type of robbers, men that it is a pleasure to know, and that you are not to be mentioned in the same category of the wicked men who rob the poor right and left, in what we consider civilization in the east. You only take toll from the great corporations who have plenty, and your robberies do not bring sorrow and sadness to the poor and hungry. No matter what inducements may be held out to me in the future, to join the life insurance robbers, the political robbers, the great corporations that wring the last dollar from their victims, I shall always remember, in declining such overtures, that I am an honorary member of this organization of honest, straightforward, conscientious holdup men, who would rob only the rich and divide with the poor, and I hope some day, if our country goes to the dogs, so a respectable man cannot hold office, or do business on the square, to come back here and become one of you in fact, and work the game to the limit. If you find you cannot make it pay out here, come east and I will give you the three-card monte and the shell game concession with our show next summer, where you can make a good living out of the jays that patronize us, and always have a little money left when we get through with them, which it is a shame for them to be allowed to carry home after the evening performance. I thank you, gentlemen."

Then the loving cup was passed, we saddled our horses and the robbers guided us in the dark through the valley, and out towards the railroad, pa's saddlebags filled with the tainted money. At daylight the next morning, when the guides left us, Pa took a big roll of bills out of his saddlebags and opened it and, by gosh, if it wasn't a lot of old confederate money that wasn't worth a cent. Pa used some words that made me sick, and then I cried. So did pa.

CHAPTER VII.

Pa and the Bad Boy Stop Off at a Lively Western Town — Pa
Buys Mining Stock and Takes Part in a Rabbit Drive.

Well, we are on the way back home, after having engaged Indians, cowboys, rough riders and highway robbers to join our show for next season. Pa felt real young and kitteny when we cam to the railroad, after leaving our robber friends at the Hole-in-the-Wall, far into the mountain country. We came to a lively town on the railroad, where every other house is a gambling house, and every other one a plain saloon, and there was great excitement in the town over our arrival, 'cause there don't very many rich and prosperous people stop there.

Pa had looked over the money the robbers had given him, to throw it away, because it was old-fashioned confederate money, when he found that there was only one bundle of confederate money, and the rest was all good greenbacks, the bundle of confederate money probably having been shipped west to some museum, and the robbers having got hold of it in the dark, brought it along. Pa burned up the bad money at the hotel, and then he got stuck on the town, and said he would stay there a few days and rest up, and incidentally break a few faro banks, by a system, the way the smart alecks break the bank at Monte Carlo.

I teased Pa to take the first train for home, so we could join the circus before it closed the season, and he could report to the managers the result of his business trip to the west, but Pa said he had heard of a man who had a herd of buffalo on a ranch not far from that town, and before he returned to the show he was going to buy a herd of buffalo for the cowboys and Indians to chase around the wild west show.

I couldn't do anything with pa, so we stayed at that town until pa got good and ready to go home. He bucked the faro bank some, but the gamblers soon found he had so much money that he could break any bank, so they closed up their lay-outs and began to sell pa mining stock in mines which were fabulously rich if they only had money to develop them. They salted some mines near town for Pa to examine, and when he found that they contained gold enough in every shovelful of dirt to make a man crazy, he bought a whole lot of stock, and then the gamblers entertained Pa for all that was out.

They got up dances and fandangos, and Pa was it, sure, and I was proud of him, cause he did not lose his head. He just acted dignified, and they thought they were entertaining a distinguished man. Everything would have gone all right, and we would have got out with honor, if it hadn't been for the annual rabbit drive that came off while we were there. Part of the country is irrigated, and good crops are grown, but the jackrabbits are so numerous that they come in off the plains adjoining the green spots, at night, and eat everything in sight, so once a year the people get up a rabbit drive and go out in the night by the hundred, on horseback, and surround the country for ten miles or so, and at daylight ride along towards a corral, where thousands of rabbits are driven in and slaughtered with clubs. The men ride close together, with dogs, and no guilty rabbit can escape,

Pa thought it would be a picnic, and so we went along, but pa wishes that he had let well enough alone and kept out of the rabbit game. Those natives are full of fun, and on these rabbit drives they always pick out some man to have fun with, and they picked out Pa as the victim. We rode along for a couple of hours, flushing rabbits by the dozen, and they would run along ahead of us, and multiply, so that when the corral was in sight ahead the prairie was alive with long eared animals, so the earth seemed to be moving, and it almost made a man dizzy to look at them.

The hundreds of men on horseback had come in close together from all sides, and when we were within half a mile of the corral the crowd stopped at a signal, and the leader told Pa that now was the time to make a cavalry charge on the rabbits, and he asked Pa if he was afraid and wanted to go back, and Pa said he had been a soldier and charged the enemy; had been a politician and had fought in hot campaigns; had hunted tigers and lions in the jungle, and rode barebacked in the circus, and gone into lions' dens, and been married, and he guessed he was not going to show the white feather chasing jackrabbits. They could sound the bugle charge as soon as they got ready, and they would find him in the game till the curtain was rung down.

That was what they wanted Pa to say, so, as pa's horse was tired, they suggested that he get on to a fresh horse, and Pa said all right, they couldn't get a horse too fresh for him, and he got on to a spunky pony, and I noticed that there was no bit in the pony's mouth, but only a rope around the pony's nose, and I was afraid something would happen to pa. I told him he and I better dismount, and climb a mesquite tree and watch the fun from a safe place.

Pa said: "Not on your life; your Pa is going right amongst the big game, and is going to make those rabbits think the day of judgment has arrived. Give me a club."

The leader handed Pa an ax handle, and when we looked ahead towards the corral where the rabbits had been driven, it seemed as though there were a million of them, and they were jumping over each other so it looked as though there was a snow bank of rabbits four feet thick. When Pa said he was ready a fellow sounded a bugle, and pa's pony started off on the jump for the corral, and all the other horses started, and everybody yelled, but they held back their horses so Pa could have the whole field to himself.

Gee, but I was sorry for pa. His horse rushed right into the corral amongst the rabbits, and when it got right where the rabbits were the thickest, the darn horse began to buck, and tossed Pa in the air just as though he had been thrown up in a blanket, and he came down on a soft bed of struggling and scared rabbits, and the other horsemen stopped at the edge of the corral and watched pa, and I got off my horse and climbed up on a post of the corral and tried to pick out pa. Then all the hundred or more dogs were let loose in amongst Pa and the rabbits, and it was a sight worth going miles to see if it had been somebody else than Pa that was holding the center of the stage, and all the crowd laughing at pa, and yelling to him to stand his ground.

Well, Pa swung his ax handle and killed an occasional rabbit, but there were thousands all around, and Pa seemed to be wading up to his middle in rabbits, and they would jump all over him, and bunt him with their heads, and scratch him with their toenails, and the dogs would grab rabbits and shake them, and Pa would fall down and rabbits would run over him till you couldn't see Pa at all. Then he would raise up again and maul the animals with his club, and his clothes were so covered with rabbit hair that he looked like a big rabbit himself. He lost his hat and looked as though he was getting exhausted, and then he stopped and spit on his hands and yelled to the rest of the men, who had dismounted and were lined up at the edge of the corral, and said: "You condemned loafers, why don't you come in here and help us dogs kill off these vermin, cause I don't want to have all the fun. Come on in, the water is fine," and Pa laughed as though he was in swimming and wanted the rest of the gang to come in.

The crowd thought they had given the distinguished stranger his inning, and so they all rushed in with clubs and began to kill rabbits and drive them away from pa. In an hour or so the most of them were killed, and Pa was so tired he went and sat down on the ground to rest, and I got down off my perch and went to Pa and asked him what he thought of this latest experience, and I began to pick rabbit hairs off pa's clothes.

"I'll tell you what it is, Hennery," said pa, as he breathed hard, as though he had been running a foot race, "this rabbit drive reminds me of the way the rich corporations look upon the poor people, just as we look upon the jackrabbits. We pity a single jackrabbit, and he runs when he sees us, and seems to say: 'Please, mister, let me alone, and let me nibble around and eat the stuff you do not want, and we drive them into a bunch, the way the rich and mean iron-handed trusts drive the people, and then we turn in and club them with the ax handle of graft and greed, and we keep our power over them, if enough are killed off so we are in the majority, but the jackrabbits that escape the drive keep on breeding, like the poor people that the trusts try to exterminate. Some day the jackrabbit and the poor people will get nerve enough to fight back, and then the jackrabbit and the poor people will outnumber the men who fight them and kill them, and they will turn on the cowboys with the clubs, and the trusts with the big head, and drive those who now pursue them into corrals on the prairies and into penitentiaries in the states, and those who are pig-headed and cruel will get theirs, see?"

I told Pa I thought I could see, though there were rabbit hairs in my eyes, and then I got Pa to get up and mount his horse, and we rode back to town with the gang, while the 5,000 rabbit carcasses were hauled to town in wagons and loaded on the cars.

"Where do you send those jackrabbits?" asked Pa of the leader of the slayers, as he watched them loading the rabbits.

"To the Chicago packing houses," said the man. "They make the finest canned chicken you ever et."

"The devil, you say," said pa. "Then we have been working all day to make packing houses rich. Wouldn't that skin you?"

Then we went to the hotel and I put court-plaster on Pa where the rabbits had scratched the skin off, and Pa arranged to go out next day to the ranch where the herd of buffaloes live, to look for bigger game for the show, though he would like to have a rabbit drive in the circus ring next year if he could train the rabbits.

CHAPTER VIII.

Pa and the Bad Boy Visit a Buffalo Ranch — Pa Pays for the Privilege of Killing a Buffalo, but Doesn't Accomplish His Purpose — He Hires a Herd for the Show Next Year.

This is the last week Pa and I will be in the far west looking for freaks for the wild west department of our show for next year. Next week, if Pa lives, we shall be back under the tent, to see the show close up the season, and shake hands all around with our old friends, the freaks, the performers, the managers and all of 'em.

It will be a glad day for us, for we have had an awful time out west. If Pa would only take advice, and travel like a plain, ordinary citizen, who is willing to learn things, it would be different, but he wants to show people that he knows it all, and he wants to pose as the one to give information, and so when he is taught anything new it jars him. Any man with horse sense would know that it takes years to learn how to rope steers, and keep from being tipped off the horse, and run over by a procession of cows, but because Pa had lassoed hitching posts in his youth, with a clothes line, with a slip noose in it, he posed among cowboys as being an expert roper, and where did he land? In the cactus.

He was just meat for the natives to have fun with, and he has sure been hashed up on this trip. But the worst of all was this trip to the buffalo ranch, to secure buffaloes for the show, and if I was in pa's place I would go into retirement, and never look a man in the face. Pa's idea was that these buffaloes on the ranch were just as wild as they used to be when they run at large on the plains. When we got to the ranch at evening, Pa put in the whole time until it was time to go to bed telling the ranchman and his hired man what great things he had done killing wild animals, and what dangerous places he had been in, and what bold things he had done. He said, while the object of his visit to the ranch was to buy a herd of buffaloes for the show, the thing he wanted to do, above all, was to kill a buffalo bull in single-handed combat, and have the head and horns to ornament his den, and the hide for a lap robe, but the ranchmen would be welcome to the meat. He asked the man who owned the ranch if he might have the privilege, by paying for it, of killing a buffalo.

The ranchman said he would arrange it all right in the morning, and Pa and I went to bed. After Pa got to snoring, and killing buffaloes in his sleep, I could hear the ranchman and his helpers planning pa's humiliation, and when I tried to tell Pa in the morning that the crowd were stringing him he got mad at me and asked me to mind my own business, and that is something I never could do to save my life.

Well, about daylight we were all out on the veranda, and they gave Pa instructions about what he was to do. The ranchman said it was against the state laws to kill buffalo, except in self-defense, so Pa would have to get in a blind, like the German emperor, and have the game driven to him. They gave Pa two big revolvers, loaded with blank cartridges, I know, because I heard them whisper about it the night before, and they gave him a peck measure of salt and told him to sneak up to a little shed out in a field and conceal himself until the game came along, and then open fire, and when his buffalo fell, mortally wounded, to go out and skin it.

Pa asked what the salt was for, and they told him it was to salt the hide. Say, I knew that the place they sent Pa to wait for buffalo was where they salted the animals once a week, and started to tell pa, but the rancher called me off and told me I could go with the men and help drive the game to destruction.

We waited until the ranchman had gone out with Pa and got him nicely concealed, the way they conceal Emperor William when he slaughters stags, and Pa looked as brave as any emperor as he got his two big revolvers ready for an emergency. The ranchman told pa that he had twelve shots in the revolvers, and he better begin firing when the big bull came over the ridge, on the trail, at the head of the herd, and as the animal advanced, as he no doubt would, to keep firing until the whole 12 shots were fired, and then if the animal was not killed, to use his own judgment as to what to do, whether to run for the house, or lay down and pretend to be dead.

Pa said he expected to kill the animal before three shots had been fired, but if the worst came he could run some, but the ranchman said if he should run that the whole herd would be apt to stampede on him and run him down, and he thought Pa better lay down and let them go by.

Gee, but I pitied Pa when we got out on the prairie and found the herd. They were as tame as Jersey cows, and the old bull, the fiercest of the lot, with a head as big as a barrel, came up to the ranchman and wanted to be scratched, like a big dog, and the calves and cows came up and licked our hands. It was hard work to drive them towards pa's blind, 'cause they wanted to be petted, but the ranchman said as soon as we could get the bull up to the top of the ridge, so the old man would open fire on him, they would hurry right along to pa's blind, 'cause they always came to be salted at the signal of a revolver shot.

So we pushed them along up towards the ridge, out of sight of pa, by punching them, and slapping them on the hams, and finally the head of the old bull appeared above the ridge on the regular cattle trail, and not more than ten rods from where Pa was concealed. Then we heard a shot and we knew Pa was alive to his danger.

"There she blows," said the ranchman, and then there was another shot, and by that time the whole herd of about 20 was on the ridge, and the shots came thick, and the herd started on a trot for the shed where Pa was, to get their salt. When we had counted 12 shots and knew pa's guns were empty we showed up on the ridge, and watched pa.

He started to run, with the peck measure of salt, but fell down and spilled the salt on the grass, and before he could get up the bull was so near that he dassent run, so he laid down and played dead, and the buffaloes surrounded him and licked up the salt, and paid no more attention to him than they would to a log until they had licked up all the salt. Then the bull began to lick pa's hands and face, and Pa yelled for help, but we got behind the ridge and went around towards the ranch, the ranchman telling us that the animals were perfectly harmless and that as soon as they had licked pa's face a little they would go off to a water hole to drink, and then go out and graze.

We left Pa yelling for help, and I guess he was praying some, 'cause once he got on his knees, but a couple of pet buffalo calves, that one of the rancher's boys drives to a cart, went up to Pa and began to lick his bald head, and chew his hair.

Well, we got around to the ranch house, where we could, see the herd, and see Pa trying to push the calves away from being so familiar, and then the herd all left Pa and went back over the ridge, and Pa was alone with his empty revolvers and the peck measure. Pa seemed to be stunned at first, and then we all started out to rescue him, and he saw us coming, and he came to meet us.

Pa was a sight. His hair was all mussed up, and his face was red and sore from contact with the rough buffaloes' tongues, and the salt on their tongues made it smart, and his coat sleeves and trousers legs had been chewed off by the buffaloes, and he looked as though he had been through a corn shredder, and yet he was still brave and noble, and as we got near to him he said:

"Got any trailing dogs?"

"What you want trailing dogs for?" asked the ranchman. "What you want is a bath. Have any luck this morning buffaloing?"

"Well I guess yes," said pa, as he dropped the peck measure, and got out a revolver and asked for more cartridges. "I put twelve bullets into that bull's carcass when he was charging on me, and how he carried them away is more than I know. Get me some dogs and a Winchester rifle and I will follow him till he drops in his tracks. That bull is my meat, you hear me?" and Pa bent over and looked at his chewed clothes.

"You don't mean to tell me the bull charged on you and didn't kill you?" said the ranchman, winking at the hired man. "How did you keep from being gored?"

"Well it takes a pretty smart animal to get the best of me," said pa, looking wise. "You see, when the bull came over the hill I gave him a couple of shots, one in the eye and another in the chest, but he came on, with his other eye flashing fire, and the hair on his head and on his hump sticking up like a porcupine, and the whole herd followed, bellowing and fairly shaking the earth, but I kept my nerve. I shot the bull full of lead, and he tottered along towards me, bound to have revenge, but just as he was going to gore me with his wicked horns I caught hold of the long hair on his head and yelled 'Get out of here, condemn you,' and I looked him in the one eye, like this," and Pa certainly did look fierce, "and he threw up his head, with me hanging to his hair, and when I came down I kicked him in the ribs and he gave a grunt and a mournful bellow, as though he was all in, and was afraid of me, and went off over the hill, followed by the herd, scared to death at a man that was not afraid to stand his ground against the fiercest animal that ever trod the ground. Now, come on and help me find the carcass." Pa looked as though he meant it.

"Well, you are a wonder," said the ranchman, looking at Pa in admiration. "I have seen men before that could lie some, but you have got Annanias beaten a block. Now we will go to the house and settle this thing, and I will send my trusty henchmen out henching after your bull."

Then we went to the house and got dinner, and the men drove up the buffalo into the barnyard and fed them hay, and we went out and played with the buffaloes, and Pa found his bull hadn't a scratch on him, and that he would lean up against Pa and rub against him just like he was a fencepost.

The ranchman told Pa they had been stringing him, and that the animals were so tame you could feed them out of your hand, and that he had been shooting blank cartridges, and the only thing he regretted was that Pa would lie so before strangers. Then pa bought the herd for the show, and next year Pa will show audiences how he can tame the wildest of the animal kingdom, so they will eat out of his hand.

CHAPTER IX

The Bad Boy and His Pa Return to the Circus to Find They Have Been Quite Forgotten — The Fat Lady and the Bearded Woman Give Pa the Cold Shoulder — Pa Finally Makes Himself Recognized and Attends the Last Performance of the Season.

We arrived from the far west and struck the show at Indianapolis, where it was playing its last date of the season, before going to winter quarters. It was a sad home coming, 'cause the animals and the performers had forgotten us, and we had to be introduced to everybody.

We arrived about noon and while I stayed down town to get a shine, Pa took a street car and went right up to the lot, and the crowd was around the ticket wagon getting ready to go in. Pa went up to the ticket taker at the entrance and said, "hello, Bill," and was going to push right in, when Bill said that was no good, and there couldn't any old geezer play the "hello Bill" business on him.

A couple of bouncers took Pa by the elbows and fired him out, and the crowd laughed at pa, and told him to go and buy a ticket like a man, and Pa told the bouncers he would discharge them on the spot. Pa went to the manager's tent and complained that he had been fired out, and the manager said that was perfectly proper, unless he had a ticket, and he told Pa to get out. Pa told them who he was, but they wouldn't believe him. You see pa's face was all red and sore where the buffaloes had licked him, and the buffaloes had licked all the hair dye out of his hair and whiskers, and they were as white as the driven snow. Pa looked 20 years older than when he went west. While they were arguing about Pa and examining him to see if he had smallpox, I came up and Pa saw me and he said, "Hennery, ain't I your pa?" and I said "you can search me, that's what they always said," and then I identified pa, and they all shook hands with him, and he reported about the trip to the west, and what talent he had engaged for the wild west department for next year. Then we all went into the tent. I guess everybody was mad and excited, 'cause the show was going to close, and the salaries stop, as some of the performers were crying, and everybody was packed up, and all were paying borrowed money.

Pa went up to the freak's platform and tapping the fat lady on the shoulder he said, "Hello, you seem to be taking on flesh, now that the show is going to close, and you ought to have got that flesh on earlier in the season."

I shall never forget the scene. The fat lady did not recognize pa, but thought he was just an ordinary old Hoosier trying to take liberties with her, and she kicked pa's feet out from under him, and pulled him down across her lap and with her big fat hand she gave him a few spanks that made Pa see stars, and then cuffed pa's ears, and let him up. He went over to the bearded woman for sympathy, asked her how she had got along without him so long; and she got mad too and swatted Pa with her fist, and yelled for help. The giant came and was going to break Pa in two, and Pa asked the giant what it was to him, and he said the bearded woman was his wife, and that they were married the week before at Toledo. The giant lifted Pa one with his hind foot, and Pa got down off the platform, and he told them that was their last season with the show, when they had no respect for the general manager.

Then they all found out who Pa was, and apologized and tried to square themselves, but Pa was hot enough to boil over, and we went off to see the animals.

Say, there wasn't a single animal that would have Pa around. The zebras kicked at pa, the lions roared and sassed him, the hyenas snarled and howled, the wolves looked ugly, and the tigers acted as though they wanted to get him in the cage and tear out his tenderloin; the elephants wanted to catch Pa and walk on his frame. The only friends Pa seemed to have was the sacred bull and cow, who let him come near them, and when they began to lick pa's hand he remembered his experience with the buffaloes, and he drew away to the monkey cages. The ourang outang seemed to look on pa as an equal, and the monkeys treated me like a long lost brother.

It was the saddest home coming I ever participated in, and

when the performance began Pa and I went and sat on the lowest seat near the ring, and the performers guyed Pa for a Hoosier, and the lemonade butchers tried to sell Pa lemonade and peanuts, which was the last hair, until a fakir tried to get Pa to bet on a shell game, and that was the limit.

Pa got up with a heavy heart, and started to go into the dressing room, and was arrested by one of the detectives, and put out under the canvas, and we went down town almost heartbroken, I told Pa to go to a barber shop and have his hair and whiskers colored black again, and put on his old checkered vest, and big plug hat, and two-pound watch chain, and they would all know him. So Pa had his hair and whiskers colored natural, and dressed up in the old way, and at evening we went back and stood around the tent, and everybody took off their hats to him, and when we went into the show at night everybody was polite, the freaks wanted Pa to sit on the platform with them, and the animals came off their perch, and treated Pa like they used to, and he was himself again.

He went around the big tent and watched the last performance of the season, and complimented the performers, went into the dressing room and jollied the members of the staff, and when the performance was over, and the audience had gone, all the managers and everybody connected with the show gathered in the ring to bid each other good bye, and make presents to each other. Everybody made speeches congratulating the management and all who had helped to make the show a success, and they all joined hands around the ring and sang "Auld Lang Sine," the animals in the next tent joining in the chorus.

The lights were lowered, and the canvas-men took down the tents and loaded them on the cars for home. We went down to the hotel and the managers listened to the reading of a statement from the treasurer showing how much money we had made, Pa drew his share of the profits, and we took a train for home.

At breakfast the next morning in the dining car, going into Chicago, Pa said to me, "Hennery, we have had the most exciting five months of my life. The circus business is just like any other business. If you make good and we are ahead of the game, it is respectable, but if you run behind and have to deal with the sheriff, you are suspected of being crooked. Make the people laugh and forget their troubles, and you are a benefactor, but if your show is so bad that it makes them kick and find fault, and wish they had stayed at home, you might as well put crape on the grand entrance, and go out of the business. The animals in a show are just like the people we meet in society. If you put on a good front, and act as though you were the whole thing, they respect you, and allow you to stay on the earth, but if you are changeable, and look different from your customary appearance, and come up to the cage in a frightened manner, they pipe you off and give you the ha, ha! See? Now we will go home and get acquainted."

"Well, pa," said I, looking him straight in the eye, "where are we going next?"

CHAPTER X.

*The Bad Boy Calls on the Old Groceryman and Gets
Acquainted with His New Dog — Off Again to See America.*

The old groceryman was sitting in the old grocery one fine spring morning looking over his accounts, as they were written on a quire of brown wrapping paper with a blunt lead pencil, and wondering where he could go to collect money to pay a note that was due at the bank at noon on that day. He was looking ten years older than he did the year before when the Bad Boy had played his last trick on the old man, and gone abroad to chaperone his sick father, in a search for health and adventure. The old man had missed the boy around the grocery, and with no one to keep his blood circulating, and his temperature occasionally soaring above the normal, he had failed in health, and had read with mixed feelings of joy, fear and resentment that the Bad Boy and his dad had arrived home, and he knew it could not be long before the boy would blow in, and he was trying to decide whether to meet the boy cheerfully and with a spirit of resignation, or to meet him with a club, whether to give him the glad hand, or form himself into a column of fours to drive him out when he came.

He had accumulated a terrier dog since the boy went away, to be company for the old singed cat, to hunt rats in the cellar, and to watch the store nights. The dog was barking down cellar, and the old man went down the rickety stairs to see what the trouble was, and while he was down there helping the dog to tree a rat under a sack of potatoes, the Bad Boy slipped into the store, and finding the old man absent, he crawled under the counter, curled up on a cracker box, and began to snore as the old man came up the stairs, followed by the dog, with a rat in his mouth. The old man heard the snore, and wondered if he had been entertaining a tramp unawares, when the dog dropped the rat and rushing behind the counter began to growl, and grabbed the Bad boy by the seat of his trousers and gave him a good shaking, while the boy set up a yell that caused the plaster to fall, and the old man to almost faint with excitement, and he went to the door to call a policeman, when the boy kicked the dog off, and raised up from behind the counter, causing the old cat to raise her back and spit cotton, and as the old man saw the Bad Boy he leaned against the show case and a large smile came over his face, and he said: "Gee whiz, where did you get on?"

"The porter was not in, so I turned in in the first lower berth I came to," said the Bad Boy, as he jumped over the counter and grabbed the old man by the arm and shook his hand until it ached. "Introduce me to your friend, the dog, who seems to have acquired an appetite for pants," and the Bad Boy got behind the old man and kicked at the dog, who was barking as though he had a cat on the fence.

"Get out, Tiger," said the old man, as he pushed the dog away. "You have got to get used to this young heathen," and he hugged the bright looking, well dressed boy as though he was proud of him.

"What are good fat rats selling for now?" asked the boy, as his eye fell on the rat the terrier had brought out of the cellar. "I did not know you had added a meat market to your grocery. Now, in Paris the rat business is a very important industry, but I didn't know the people ate them here. What do you retail them at?"

"O, get out, I don't sell rats," said the old man, indignantly. "I got this dog for company, in your place, and he has proved himself more useful than any boy I ever saw. Say, come and sit down by the stove, and tell me all about your trip, as your letters to me were not very full of information. How is your father's health?"

"Dad is the healthiest man in America," said the boy, as he handed the old man a Turkish cigarette, with a piece of cheese under the tobacco about half an inch from where the old man lighted it with a match. "Dad is all right, except his back. He slept four nights with a cork life preserver strapped to, his back, coming over, and he has got curvature of the spine, but the doctor has strapped a board to dad's back, and says when his back warps back to fit the board he will be sound again."

"Say, this is a genuine Turkish cigarette, isn't it," said the old man, as he puffed away at it, and blew the smoke through his nose.

"I have always wanted to smoke a genuine, imported cigarette. Got a flavor something like a Welsh rabbit, ain't it?" and the old man looked at the cigarette where the frying cheese was soaking through the paper.

"Gee, but I can't go that," and he threw it away and looked sea sick.

"Turks always take cheese in their cigarettes," said the Bad Boy. "They get a smoke and food at the same time. But if you feel sick you can go out in the back yard and I will wait for you."

"No, I will be all right," said the old man, as he got up to wait on a customer. "Here, try a glass of my cider," and he handed the boy a dirty glass half filled with cider which the boy drank, and then looked queer at the old man.

"Tastes like it smells going through the oil belt in Indiana," said the boy. "What's in it?"

"Kerosene," said the old man. "The Turks like kerosene in their cider. They get drink and light, if they touch a match to their breath. Say, that makes us even. Now, tell me, what country did you dad get robbed the most in while you were abroad?"

"Well, it was about a stand off," said the boy, as he made a slip noose on the end of a piece of twine, and was trying to make a hitch over the bob tail of the groceryman's dog, with an idea of fastening a tomato can to the string a little later, and turning the dog loose. "Do you know," said he to the old man, "that I think it is wrong to cut off a dog's tail, cause when you tie a tin can to it you feel as though you were taking advantage of a cripple.

"Well, all the countries we visited robbed dad of all the money he had, one way of another, sooner or later; even our own country, when we arrived in New York, took his roll for duty on some little things he smuggled, but I think the combination of robbers at Carlsbad stuck together and got the goods off dad in the most systematic manner. Some way they got news when we arrived, of the exact amount of money dad had got out of the bank, and before we had breakfast the fakers had divided it up among themselves, and each one knew just what was going to be his share, and it was just like getting a check from home for them. If we were going there again we would give the money to some particular faker to divide with the rest, and then take a few swallows of their rotten egg water, and get out.

"Say, did you ever eat a piece of custard pie made out of stale eggs? Well, that is just about the same as the Carlsbad water, only the water is not baked with a raw crust on the bottom. But the doctor dad consulted was the peach. Dad asked him how much of the water he ought to drink, and the doctor held a counsel with himself, and said dad might drink all he could hold, and when dad asked him how much his charges were he said, 'Oh, wait till you are cured.' So dad thought he was not going to charge for his advice, but after we had drank the water for ten days, and dad was so weak he couldn't brush the flies off his bald spot, we decided to go to rest cure, and when we had our tickets bought the doctor attached our baggage, and had a bill against dad for four hundred and sixty dollars for consultations, operations, advice, board and borrowed money, and he had a dozen witnesses to prove every item. Dad paid it, but we are going there once more with a keg of dynamite for that doctor. But dad thinks he got the worth of his money.

"You remember before he went away he thought the doctors who operated on him for that 'pendecitus' left a monkey wrench in him when they sewed him up. Well, after he began to drink that water he found iron rust on the towels when he took a bath, and he believes the monkey wrench was sweat out of him. Say, does your dog like candy?"

"O, yes, he eats a little," said the groceryman, and the boy tossed a piece of candy such as he gave the King of Spain, with cayenne pepper in it, to the dog, which swallowed it whole, and the old man said, "Now, I suppose your father is cured, you will stay at home for awhile, and settle down to decent citizenship, and take an active part in the affairs of your city and state? Gee, but what is the matter with the dog?" added the old man, as the dog jumped up on all fours, looked crosseyed, and tried to dig a hole in his stomach with his hind leg.

"O, no, we shall never stay home much more," said the Bad

Boy, getting up on a barrel and pulling his feet up to get away from the dog, which was beginning to act queer. "You see, dad got cured all right, of a few diseases that were carrying him off, but he has taken the 'jumps,' a disease that is incurable. When a man has the 'jumps' he can't stay long in one place, but his life after taking the disease is one continual round of packing up and unpacking. His literature is time cards and railroad guides, and his meals are largely taken at railroad eating houses, sitting on a stool, and his sleep is uncertain cat naps. Say, that dog acts as though the mouthful he took out of my pants under the counter didn't agree with him," added the boy, as the dog rolled over and tried to stand on his head.

"Dog does act kinder like he had something on his mind," said the old man, as he got out of the dog's way, so he could do his acrobatic stunt. "Where is your dad going next trip? Seems as though he would want to stay home long enough to change his shirt."

"Don't have to change your shirt when you travel," said the boy, as he slipped an imitation snake into the side pocket of the old groceryman's sack coat. "We are going to see all the world, now that we have started in the traveling industry, but our next move will be chasing ourselves around our own native land. Say, if you have never been vaccinated against mad dog, you better take something right now, for that dog is mad, and in about two minutes he is going to begin to snap at people, and there is no death so terrible as death from a mad dog bite. Gee, but I wouldn't be in your for a million dollars." And the boy stood upon the barrel, and was beginning to yell "mad dog," when the old man asked what he could take to make him immune from the bite of a mad dog.

"Eat a bottle of horseradish," said the boy, as he reached over to the shelves and got a bottle, and pulled the cork. "Eminent scientists agree that horseradish is the only thing that will get the system in shape to withstand and throw off the mad dog virus," and he handed the old man the bottle and he began to eat it, and cry, and choke, and the boy got down from the barrel and let the dog out doors, and he made a bee line for the lake.

"He's a water dog all right," said the boy, and as a servant girl came in to buy some soap, and saw the old man eating raw horse-radish and choking and looking apoplectic, she asked what was the matter with the old man, and a boy said a mad dog just escaped from the store, and that the old man had shown signs of madness ever since; the girl gave a yell and rushed out into the world without her soap. "Let this be a lesson to you to be kind to dumb animals," said the boy to the old man, as he finished the bottle of horseradish, and put his hands on his stomach.

"Write to me, won't you?" said the old groceryman, "and may the fiercest grizzly bear get you, and eat you, condemn you," and the old man opened the door and pointed to the street.

"Sure," said the Bad Boy. "I will write you but beware of the dog. Good-bye. You are a good thing. Push yourself along," and the Bad Boy went out to pack up for another journey.

CHAPTER XI.

The Bad Boy Relates the Automobile Ride He and Dad
Had — They Sneak Out of Town.

"Give me a package of your strongest breakfast food, and a big onion," said the Bad Boy, as he came into the grocery, looking as weak as a fever convalescent, "and I want to eat the onion right now."

"Well, that is a combination, sure enough," said the old groceryman, as he wrapped a package of breakfast food in a paper and watched the boy rub half an onion on a salt bag, and eat it greedily. "What is the matter with you to look so sick, and eat raw onion before breakfast?"

"Oh, it is this new-fashioned way of living that is killing little Hennery. When I lived at home before we used to have sassidge and pancakes for breakfast, roast meat for dinner and cold meat for supper, and dad was healthy as a tramp, ma could dance a highland fling, I could play all kinds of games and jump over a high board fence when anybody was chasing me. Now we have some kind of breakfast food three times a day because ma reads the advertisements, and dad is so weak he has to be helped to dress, ma goes moping around like a fashionable invalid, I am so tired I can't hit a window with a snowball, and the dog that used to fight cats now wants to lay in front of the grate and wish he was dead. Gosh, but there ought to be a law that any man that invents a new breakfast food should be compelled to eat it. Gee, but that onion gives a man strength."

"I should think so," said the old groceryman, as he took a rag and set it on fire and let the smoke purify the room. "But I suppose your folks are like a great many others who have quit eating meat on account of the meat trust, and are going to die in their tracks on health food. Is your dad going out today to get the fresh air and brace up for his next trip?"

"No, dad is going to stay in the house. He wants ma to get him a female trained nurse, but ma kicks. They had a trained nurse for a week, once, but ma had one of those little electric flashlights that you touch a button and it lights up the room like a burglar was in the house, and she used to get up in the night and flash the light into dad's room. Dad always had nervous prostration after ma flashed the light, and the nurse fainted dead away, so ma and I are going to do the nursing until dad is strong enough to travel again, and then he and I skip."

"Where are you going first?" asked the old groceryman, as he opened the door to let the odor of onion, and burned rag out of the room. "What kind of treatment do the doctors advise to bring the old man around so he will be himself again?"

"They want him to go where he can take baths, and gamble, and attend horse races, and go into fast society, and maybe have a fight or two so as to stir his blood, and we have decided to take him first to the hot springs and turn him loose, and we are packing up now and shall go next week. They tell me that at the Arkansaw Hot Springs you can get into any kind of a scrape you want, and you don't have to look around for trouble. It comes to you. Oh, we won't do a thing down there. I broke the news to dad last night, and he said that was good enough for him, and he has packed up his poker chips and some marked cards he used to win money with from the deacons in the church, and he wants to go as quick as possible. You will have to excuse me now, for I am going to take dad out in an automobile after breakfast to give him his first dose of excitement. I will make dad think that automobiling is a sport next to fox hunting, and I will drop in this afternoon and tell you about it," and the Bad Boy took his breakfast food and went home.

"Jerusalem, but you are a sight," said the groceryman late in the afternoon, as the bad boy came in with a pair of black goggles on, his coat torn down the back and his pants ripped up the legs. "What a time you must have had in the automobile. Did you run over anybody?"

"Everybody," said the bad boy, as he pinned his trousers leg together with a safety pin. "There they go now with dad in a milk wagon. Say, these airships that run on the ground give a man all the excitement he needs."

"Hurry up and tell me about your automobile ride," said the

groceryman as he brushed off the bad boy's clothes with an old blacking brush.

"Well, dad said he had never taken a ride in one of the devil wagons, though he had got a good deal of exercise the last year or two dodging them on the streets, but he said he was tickled to death to hear that I was an expert performer, and he would go out with me, and if he liked the sensation, he would buy one. The machine I hired was one of those doublets for two persons, one seat, you know, a runabout. It was a runabout all right. It run about eighteen miles in fifteen minutes. I got dad tucked in, and touched her on a raw spot, and we were off. I run her around town for a while on the streets that had no teams on, and dad was pleased. He said:

"'Hennery, I like a boy that knows something about machinery, and who knows what dingus to touch to make his machine do a certain thing, and I am proud of you.'

"We had to go through the business part of town, and dad looked around at the people on the streets that he knew, and he swelled up and tried to look as though he owned a brewery, and told me to let her out, and I thought if dad could stand it to let her out I could, so I pulled her open just as one of these station fruit venders with a hand cart was crossing the street. The cowcatcher in front caught the hand cart right in the middle and threw it into the air and it rained bananas and oranges, and the dago came down on his head and swore in Italian, and dad said, 'Good shot, Hennery,' and then the machine swung across the street and knocked the fender off a street car, and then I got her in the road straight and by gosh I couldn't stop her. Something had got balled up, and the more I touched things the faster she went. We frightened four teams and had three runaways, and the air seemed full of horses rearing up and drivers yelling for us to stop. One farmer with a load of hay would not give any of the road, and I guess his hay came in contact with the gasoline tank, for the hay took fire, his team ran away, and as we went over the hill I looked back and saw a fire engine trying to catch up with the red-hot load of hay, and the farmer had grabbed hold of a wire sign across the street and let the wagon run out from under him, and they had to take him down with a fire ladder.

"We kept going faster, and dad began to get frightened and asked me to slow up, but I couldn't. We must have got in the country about eight miles, and dad was getting scared, and his face was just the color of salt pork, and he said:

"'Hennery, this excursion is going to wind up in a tragedy, and if I die I want you to have a post-mortem examination made, just to see if I am right about those doctors leaving that monkey wrench in me. For heaven's sake make the machine jump that fence, for here comes a drove of cattle in the road, more'n a hundred horned steers, and we never can pass them alive.'"

"Gee, but when I saw those cattle ahead and the machine running away, I tried to pray, and then I steered her towards an old rail fence that looked as though it was rotten, and then there was a crash, the air was full of rails, and dad said, 'This is no hurdle race,' and we landed in a field where there was an old hard snow bank. She went up on the side, hit the frozen snow, turned a summersault, the gasoline tank exploded and I didn't remember anything till some farmers that were spreading manure in the field turned me over with a pitchfork and asked me who the old dead man was standing on his head in the snow bank with his plug hat around his neck. As soon as I came to I went to dad, and he was just coming out of a trance, and asked him if he didn't think a little excitement sort of made the sluggish blood circulate, and he looked at the blood on the snow, and said he thought there was no doubt about the circulation of his blood.

"He got up, got his hat untangled, told the farmers he was obliged to them for their courtesy and then he called me one side and said:

"'Hennery, this attempt on your part to murder me was not the success that you expected, but you keep on and you will get me all right. Now, as a business man, I want to say we have got to get out of this town tonight or we will be arrested and sent to the penitentiary; besides, I will have to pay a thousand dollars damage at the least calculation. Get me a carriage for home, and you stay and set this machine on fire and skip back to town in time for the evening train south, and we will go where the climate is more genial.'

"Just then the steers we saw in the road came into the field through the fence we had broken, and when they smelled the blood they began to paw and beller, and look like they would run at dad, so the farmers got dad into a milk wagon that was going to town, and when the wagon started dad was pouring a cup of milk on him where the gasoline had scorched him when it exploded, and I walked in town helping the fellows drive the steers, and here I am, alive and ready to travel at 8 p. m.

"If my chum comes around tell him I will write him from Hot Springs and give him the news."

"If that don't beat anything I ever heard of," said the old grocery man. "I have always been afraid of those automobiles, and when one of the horns blow I go in the first gate, say my prayers and wait for it to go by and run over some one farther down the block. Did your dad say anything about buying an automobile after he came to?"

"Yes, as I remember it, he said he would see me in hell first, or something like that. He remarked, as he got in the milk wagon, that every man that owned an automobile ought to be examined by an insanity expert and sent to the penitentiary for letting concealed weapons carry him.

"Well, good-by, old man," and the bad boy went limping out of the grocery to go home and tell his mother that he and dad had been scoring up for the good time they were going to have when they got out on the road for dad's health.

CHAPTER XII.

The Bad Boy Writes His Chum Not to Get So Gay — Dad's
Experience with the Pecarries.

"Hot Springs, Ark. — My dear old chum: Dad and I got here three days ago, and have begun to enjoy life. We didn't leave home a minute too soon, as we would have been arrested for running over that banana peddler, and for arson in setting a load of hay on fire and destroying the farmer's pants in our automobile accident. Ma writes that a policeman and a deputy sheriff have camped on our front doorstep ever since we left, waiting for dad and I to show up. Dad wants me to tell you to notify the officers that they can go plum, as we shall never come back. Tell them we have gone to Panama, or Mexico, or any old place.

"By the way, kid, I shall have to give you a little fatherly advice. When dad and I were at the bank getting a wad to travel with, I asked one of the clerks how it was that the bank dispensed with your services, after you had been there nearly a year, and had got your salary up to $60 a month, and were just becoming worth your salt. He said you got too fresh, that every new responsibility that was put upon you caused your chest to swell, and that you walked around as though you were president of the bank, and that you got ashamed to carry your lunch to the bank, to eat it in the back room, but went out to a restaurant and ordered the things to eat that came under the 15-cent list, whether you liked the food or not, just to show off; and instead of quietly eating the wholesome lunch your mother put up for you, and being good natured, you ate the restaurant refuse, and got cross, and all for style, showing that you had got the big head; and that you demanded an increase of salary, like a walking delegate, and got fired, as you ought to have been; and now you are walking on your uppers, and are ashamed to look into the bank, which you think is going to fail because you have withdrawn your support. Dad arranged with the managers to take you back on probation, so you go and report for duty just as though you had been off on a vacation, and then you try and have some sense. Dad says you should get to the bank before you are expected, and stay a little while after it is time to quit, and don't watch the clock and get your coat on before it strikes, and don't make a center rush for the door, as though you were escaping from jail. Let those above you see that there is not enough for you to do, and that you are anxious to help all around the place. Look upon a bale of money just as you would look upon a bale of hay if you were working in a feed store, and don't look covetous upon a pile of bills, and wonder how much there is in it, and think how much you could buy with it if it was yours. It is just a part of the business, that pile of money is, and it is not your place to brood over it with venom in your eyes, or some day you will reach out and take a little, and look guilty, and if they don't find you out, you will take a bigger slice next time, and go and blow yourself for clothes as good as the president of the bank wears, and some night you will open a small bottle of wine, and put your thumbs in the arm-holes of your vest and imagine you are 'it,' and when you flash your roll to pay the score, the quiet man at another table in the saloon, who has been drinking pop, and whom you were sorry for, he looked so forlorn, will take you into the police station, and they will search you, and you will break down and blubber, and then it is all off, and the next day you will be before a judge, and your broken-hearted mother will be there trying to convince the judge that somebody must have put the money in your pocket to ruin you, some one jealous of your great success as a banker, but the judge will know how you came by the money, and you will go over the road, your mother goes to the grave, and your friends will say it is a pity about you.

"Men who employ boys know that half of them will never amount to a tinker's dam, a quarter of them will just pass muster, and if they can't run the place in a year they will find another job, and two out of the 20 will be what are needed in the business. The boy who is always looking for another job is the one that never finds one that suits him. The two boys out of the twenty will seem to look a little rustier each year as to clothes but their round, rosy faces will change from year to year, the jaws begin to show strength, the eyes get to looking through you, and the forehead seems to expand as the brain gets to working.

"The successful boys out of the bunch remind me of the automatic repeating rifle, that you put ten cartridges in and pull the trigger and shoot ten times with your eyes shut, if you want to, and it hits where you point it. Every time an employer pulls the trigger on a successful business boy, and a good idea of business is fired, the recoil puts a new idea into the chamber, and you pull again, and so on until the magazine of the brainy boy is emptied, when you load him up again, and he is ready for business, and the employer wouldn't be without him, and would not go back to the old-fashioned one-idea boy, that goes off half-cocked when not pointed at anything in particular, and whose ideas get stuck in the barrel and have to be pulled out with a wormer, and primed with borrowed powder, and touched off by the neighbors, most of whom get powder in their eyes, unless they look the other way when the useless employee goes off, for anything in the world. So, chum, you go back to the bank and become an automatic repeater in business, with ideas to distribute to others, instead of borrowing ideas, and you will own the bank some day.

"Now, kid, you don't want to go peddling this around among the neighbors, but dad and I are having the time of our lives here, and since dad has begun to get acquainted with the ladies here at the hotel, and the millionaire sports, he is getting well, and acts like old times. He sat in the parlor of the hotel with a widow the first night until the porter had to tell him to cut it out. Say, I got asleep three or four times on a lounge in the parlor, waiting for dad to get to the 'continued in our next' in talking with that widow about his wealth, and his loneliness since ma died. He said he didn't know what he was worth, because he didn't pay any attention to any of his bonds and securities, except his Standard Oil stock, because the dividends on that stock came regular and increased a little every quarter.

Gee, but I wanted to tell her that all the interest he had in Standard Oil was a gallon kerosene can with a potato stuck in the spout, and when we went to bed I told him that woman's husband was behind the door of the parlor all the time listening, and he had a gun in his hip pocket, and would call him out for a duel the next morning, sure. Dad didn't sleep good that night, and the next morning I got a gambler to look cross at dad and size him up, and dad didn't eat any breakfast. After breakfast I had the hotel stenographer write a challenge to dad, and demand satisfaction for alienating the affections of his wife, and dad began to get weak in the knees. He showed me the challenge, and I told him the only way to do in this climate was to walk around and punch his cane on the floor, and look mad, and talk loud, and the challenger would know he was a fiery fighter, and would apologize, and dad walked around town and through the hotel office most of the day, fairly frothing at the mouth, and he thinks he has scared the challenger away, and, as the woman is gone, dad thinks he is a hero.

"But the worst thing has happened and it will take a week to grow new skin on dad's legs. He got acquainted with a bunch of men who were bear hunters and sports, and they talked of the bear shooting in Arkansas, and dad told about how he had killed tigers, lions, elephants and things until they thought he was great. Dad never saw one of those animals except in a menagerie, but when they suggested that he go with them on a bear hunt, he bit like a bass, and the whole bunch went off in a buckboard one morning with guns, lunches, hounds, bottles, and all kinds of ammunition. They didn't let me go but when the crowd came back about midnight, and they carried dad up to his room, and sent for a doctor, one of the horse race men who went along told me all about it.

"He said they went out in a canebrake and stationed dad on a runway for bear, and put in the dogs about a mile away in the swamp, and they left him there for five hours, and when they went to where he was, there was a drove of wild hogs, or peccaries, under a tree, and dad was up, on a limb praying, his gun on the ground; his coat was chewed by the wild pigs, and the wild animals were jumping up to eat his shoes. The fellows hid behind trees and listened to dad confess his sins, and pray, and promise to do better, and be a good man, and when a wild pig would gnash his teeth and make a jump at him, he would talk swear words at the pig, and then he would put up his hands and ask forgiveness, and promise to lead a different life, and say what a fool he was to be off down here in the sunny south being eaten alive by wild hogs, when he ought to be home enjoying religion. Just as dad was about to die there on the limb of a shagbark hickory, the fellows behind the trees touched off a small dynamite cartridge and threw it under the tree, and when it exploded the wild hogs ran away, dad fell off the limb, and he was rescued. He was a sight, for sure, when they brought him to the hotel; his clothes were torn off, his stomach lacerated, and when he was stuck together with plasters, and I was alone with him, he said he was as good a bear hunter as ever came down the pike, but he never worked in a slaughter house, and didn't know anything about slaughtering pigs, and besides, if he ever got out again, and able to use a gun, he would put that bunch of hunters that took him out in the canbrakes under the sod. He said while he sat up the tree praying for strength to endure the ordeal he had a revelation that there wasn't a bear within a hundred miles, and that those fellows had the hogs trained to scare visitors to Hot Springs, so they could be easy to rob. He said one fellow borrowed $50 off him to pay into the state treasury for wear and tear on the wild hogs. Well, dad had forgotten about the monkey-wrench in his system, and I guess we are going to enjoy ourselves here in the old-fashioned way. Yours all right,

"Hennery."

CHAPTER XIII.

The Bad Boy and His Dad Have Trouble with a New Breakfast Food — Dad Rides a Bucking Broncho.

San Antonio, Texas. — My Dear Chum: Dad and I left Hot Springs because the man who kept the hotel where we stopped got prejudiced against me. I suppose I did carry the thing a little too far. You see dad has got into this breakfast food habit, and reads all the advertisements that describe new inventions of breakfast food, and he has got himself so worked up over the bran mash that he is losing appetite for anything substantial, and he is getting weak and nutty. Ma told me when I went away with dad that she wanted me to try my best to break dad of the breakfast food habit, and I promised to do it. Say, kid, if you ever expect to succeed in life, you have got to establish a reputation for keeping your promises. Truth is mighty, and when anybody can depend upon a boy to do as he agrees his fortune is made. Dad saw a new breakfast food advertised in an eastern magazine, and as the hotel people only kept thirty or forty kinds of mockingbird food for guests, dad made me go out to the groceries and round up the new kind. I brought a box to the table at breakfast, and dad fell over himself to fill his saucer, and then he offered some to eight boarders that sat at our table. Dad had been bragging for a week about how he had adopted the breakfast food fad, first for his health, and then to get even with the beef trust. He had convinced the boarders at our table that it was a patriotic duty of every citizen to shut down on eating meat until the criminal meat trust was ruined.

"The breakfast food I put up on dad was some pulverized cork that I got at a grocery out of a barrel of California grapes. It looked exactly like other breakfast food, but you'd a died to see dad and several invalid Southern colonels, and two women who were at the table, pour cream on that pulverized cork, and springle sugar on it, and try to get the pulverized cork to soak up the cream, but the particles of cork floated on top of the cream, and acted alive. An old confederate colonel, who had called dad a dam yankee ever since we had been there, and always acted as though he was on the point of drawing a gun, took the first mouthful, and after chewing it a while he swallowed as though his throat was sore, but he got it down, and ordered a cocktail, and looked mad at dad. Dad noticed that the others were having difficulty in masticating the food, and so he pitched in and ate his food and said it was the finest he ever tasted, but the rest of the crowd only took a spoonful or two, and et fruit. One woman who is there to be cured of the habit of betting on the races, got the cork in amongst her false teeth and it squeaked when she chewed, like pulling a cork out of a beer bottle. They all seemed to want to please dad, and so they munched away at the cork, until the woman with the false teeth had to leave the table, then a colonel went out, and then all quit the table except dad and I, and by that time dad felt as though he had swallowed a life preserver, and he said to me:

"'Hennery, either the baths or the climate, or something has upset me, and I feel as though your dad was not very long for this world. Before I die I want you to confess to me what that stuff is that I have been eating, and I can die in peace!'

"I told him that he had wanted a light breakfast, and I though there was nothing quite so light as cork, and that he was full clear to the muzzle with pulverized cork, and he couldn't sink any more when he took a bath. Dad turned pale and we went out in the office and found that all the people who sat at our table, and ate breakfast food were in the hands of doctors, and dad went in the room with them, and each had a doctor, and how they got it out of them I don't know, as I was busy organizing a strike among the bell boys. I told them they could double their wages by striking at exactly at ten o'clock, when all the boarders wanted cocktails sent to their rooms.

"They struck all right, and the breakfast food people had all got pumped out, and then it came my turn. Dad gave me a licking, the boarders kicked at me, the landlord ordered me out of the house, and the striking bell boys who had their places filled in ten minutes, chased me all over town, and when I got back to the hotel dad had bought tickets to San Antonio, because the doctor told him to get out on the prairies and take horseback exercise to shake the pulverized cork and the monkey-wrench out of his system, and everybody threw stones at the buss that we rode to the depot in. Gosh, but I hate a town where genius has no chance against the mob element. The worst was that woman with the false teeth, because she lost them somewhere, and had to hold her handkerchief over her mouth while she called me names when the porter took me by the collar and the pants and flung me into the buss. Dad told the porter, when he handed out the regular 'tip,' that he would have made it large if the porter had taken an axe to me. Dad is getting so funny he almost makes me laugh.

"Well, kid, we arrived here next day, and got acclimated before night. Dad bought a wide gray cowboy hat, with a leather strap for a band, and began to pose as a regular old rough rider, and told everybody at the hotel that he was going to buy a ranch, and run for congress. Everybody here is willing a northern man should buy a ranch, but when he talks about running for Congress they look sassy at him, but dad can look just as sassy as anybody here. He told all around that he was a cavalry veteran of the war, and wanted to get a horse to ride that would stir up his patriotic instincts and his liver, and all his insides, and a real kind man steered dad to a livery stable, and I knew by the way the natives winked at each other that they were going to let him have a horse that would jounce him all right.

"They saddled up a real nice pony for me, but when they led out the horse for dad I knew that trouble was coming. The horse was round shouldered on the back, and when they put the saddle on the horse humped up and coughed most pitiful, and when they fastened the cinch the horse groaned and the crowd all laughed, A negro boy asked me if my old man was ever on a horse before, and when I told him that dad had eaten horses in the army, the boy said that horse would eat him, 'cause he was a bucker from Buckersville in the western part of the state.

I told dad the horse was a dangerous bucker, but he tipped his hat on one side and said he had broken more bucking bronchos than those Texas livery men ever saw. Dad borrowed a pair of these

Mexican spurs with a wheel in them as big as a silver dollar, and the men held the horse by the bridle while dad got on, and I must say he got on like he knew how. He asked which was the road to Houston, and we started out of town.

"Well, sir, I have been in a good many runaways, and I was filling a soda fountain once when it exploded, and I have been on a toboggan when it run into a cow, and I have been to a church sociable when a boy turned some rats loose, and a terrier went after them right among the women, but I never was so paralyzed as I was to see dad and that horse try to stay together. The first two miles out of town the horse walked, and acted as though it was going to die, and my pony would get away ahead and have to wait for dad and the camel to come up. Dad was mad because they gave him such a slow horse.

"'What are those things on your heels for?' I says to dad. 'Why don't you run the spokes into his slats?' I said, just to be sociable.

"'Never you mind me,' says dad. 'After I have looked at the scenery a while I will open the throttle on this dromedary, and we will go and visit the Pyramids.'

"I was a little ahead and I did not catch dad in the act of kicking open the throttle, but I heard something that sounded like a freight train wreck, and dad and the horse went by me like a horse race, only that horse was not on the ground half the time, and he didn't go straight ahead, but just lowered his head between his legs and jumped in the air and came down stifflegged and then jumped sideways, and changed ends and did it all over again, all over the prairie, and dad was a sight. His eyes stuck out, and his teeth rattled, and every time the horse came down on his feet dad seemed to get shorter, as though his spine was being telescoped up into his hat. I think dad would have fallen off the first jump, only he had rammed the spurs in amongst the horse's ribs, and couldn't get them out. Gee, but you never saw such actions, unless you have seen a horse go plum crazy. The horse kept giving dad new fancy side steps, and jumps until dad yelled to me to get a gun and shoot him or the horse, and he didn't care which. I yelled to dad to loosen up on the bridle, and let the horse run lengthways instead of sideways, and I guess he did, for the horse lit out for some musquite trees and before I could get there the horse had run under a limb and scraped dad off, and when I got there dad was lying under a tree, trying to pray and swear all to wonst, and his spurs were all blood and hair, and things a horse wears on the inside of his self, and the horse was standing not far away, eating grass, and looking at dad. If dad had had his revolver along he would have killed the horse, but the horse seemed to know he had been fooling with an unarmed man. I got dad righted up, and he rode my pony to town, and I had to lead the bucking horse, and he eat some of the cloth out of my pants.

"Say, this is a bully place down here; just as quiet and sunshiny as can be, only dad is in a hospital for a week or so, having operations on where the horse let him drop once in a while on the saddle, and the livery man made dad buy the horse 'cause he said dad had ripped his sides out with the spurs. Dad says we will have a picnic when he gets out of the hospital. He is going to buy some dynamite and take the horse out on the prairie and blow him up. Dad is _so_ fond of dumb animals. I got your letter about your being in love. Gee, but you can't afford it on your salary.

"Yours quite truly,
"HENNERY."

CHAPTER XIV.

The Bad Boy and his Dad Return from Texas — The Boy Tells the Groceryman About the Excitement at San Antonio.

The old groceryman sat on an upturned half bushel measure in front of the store drying his old-fashioned boots. As he fried the soles in front of the red hot stove, there was an odor of burnt leather, but he did not notice it, as the other odors natural to the dirty old grocery seemed to be in the majority. The door opened quietly and the old man got up to wait on a possible customer, when the bald boy rushed in and dropped on the floor the queerest animal the old man and the cat had ever seen. The cat got up on the counter on a pile of brown wrapping paper, curved its back and purmeyowed, and the strange animal jumped into a half barrel of dried apples and began to dig with all four feet, as though to make a bed to lie in.

"Take that animalcule, or whatever it is, out of them apples," said the old groceryman, picking up a fire-poker. "What is it, and where did it come from, and when did you get back, and how is your pa, and why didn't you stay away, and what do you want here anyway?" and the old man eyed the animal and the bad boy, expecting to be bitten by one and bilked by the other.

"That's a prairie dog from Texas, if you are not posted in ornicothology," said the boy, as he took the prairie dog up and put him on the counter near the cat. "Dad is all right, only we were driven out of Texas by the board of health."

"I told that pirate chum of yours when he read me your letter, that you would last in Texas just about a week, and that you would be shipped home in a box. They are not as tolerant with public nuisances down south as we are here. But what did you do there to get the board of health after you?" and the old man pushed the cat's back down level, and held her tail so she couldn't eat the prairie dog.

"Well, sir, it was the condemnedest outrage that ever was," said the boy, as he gave the prairie dog some crackers and cheese. "You see, dad told me I could pick up some pet animals while I was in Texas, and I got quite a collection while dad was in the hospital. Here is one in my pocket," and the boy took a horned toad out of his pocket, about as big as a soft-shelled crab, and put it in the old groceryman's hand.

"Condemn you, don't you put a poisonous reptile in my hand," said the odd man, as he dropped the ugly-looking toad on the floor, and got behind the show case, while the boy laughed fit to kill. "Now tell your story and vamoose, by ginger, or I will ring for the patrol wagon. You would murder a man in his own house, and laugh at his spasms."

"O, get out, that toad and this prairie dog are as harmless as your old cat there," said the boy, as he watched the old man tremble as though he had jim-jams. "I have got a tarantula and a diamond-back rattlesnake that will pizen you, though. I'll tell you about our getting fired out of Texas, if you will stand still a minute. You see, I had my collection of pets in my room at the hotel, and I had the bell boys bribed, and the chambermaid would only come in our room while I was there to watch the pets. The night dad got back from the hospital, where he went to grow some new bones and things on his insides, after he rode the bucking broncho, a man got me the prettiest little animal you ever saw, sort of white and black, about the size of a cat, and I took it to the room and put it under the bed in a box the man gave me. Dad had gone to bed, and was snoring so you could cut it with a knife."

"Say, you knew that animal was a skunk all the time, now tell me, didn't you," said the old groceryman. "You was a fool to take it, when you knew what a skunk will do."

"Yes, I thought it was a skunk, all right," said the boy, "but the man told me the animal had been vaccinated, and wouldn't ever make any trouble for any one, and he would warrant it. I thought a warranted skunk was all right, and so I went to bed in a cot next to dad's bed. I guess it was about daylight when skunks want to suck eggs, that he began to scratch the box, and squeak, and I was afraid it would wake dad up, so I reached down and took off the cover of the box. From that very identical moment the trouble began. Dad heard something in the room and he rose up in bed and the animal sat on the foot of the bed and looked at dad. Dad said 'scat,' and threw a pillow at my pet, and then all was chaos. I never exactly smelled chaos, but I know it when I smell it. O, O, but you'd a dide to see dad. He turned blue and green, and said, 'Hennery, someone has opened a jack pot, call for the police!' I rushed for the indicator where you ring for bell boys, and cocktails, and things, and touched all the buttons, and then got in bed and pulled a quilt over my head, and dad went into a closet where my snakes and things were, and the vaccinated skunk kept on doing the same as he did to dad, and I though I should die. Dad heard my snake rattle his self in the box, and he stepped on my prairie dog and yelled murder, and he got into my box of horned toads, and my young badger scratched dad's bare feet, and a young eagle I had began to screech, and dad began to have a fit. He said the air seemed fixed, and he opened the window, and sat on the window sill in his night shirt, and a fireman came up a ladder from the outside and turned the hose on dad, then the police came and broke in the door, and the landlord was along, and the porter, and all the chambermaids, and everybody. I had turned in all the alarms there were, and everybody came quick. The skunk met the policemen halfway, and saluted them as polite as could be, and they fell back for reinforcements; dad got into his pants and yelled that he was stabbed, and I don't know what didn't happen. Finally the policemen got my skunk under a blanket and walked on him, and he was squashed, but, by gosh, they can never use that blanket again, and I told 'em so."

"It's a wonder they didn't put a blanket over you and kill you too," said the old groceryman, as he moved away from the horned toad, which the boy had placed on the counter. "What did they do to you then? What way did your dad explain it? How long did you remain at the hotel after that?"

"We didn't stay hardly any after that," said the boy, as he pushed the prairie dog along the counter toward the groceryman's cat, hoping to get them to fighting. "The landlord said we dam yankees were too strenuous for his climate, and if we didn't get out of the house in fifteen minutes he would get a gun and see about it, and he left two policemen to see that we got away. Dad tried to argue the question with the landlord, after all the windows had been opened in the house. He said he had come to Texas for a quiet life, to get away from the climate of the north, but he had no idea any landlord would turn animals into a gentleman's room, and he would sue for damages; but the bluff did not work, and we left San Antonio on a freight train, under escort of the police, and the board of health. Say, that freight train smelled like it had a hot box, but nobody suspected us. When we got most to New Orleans dad said, 'Hennery, I hope this will be a lesson to you,' and I told him two more such lessons would kill his little boy dead."

"What did you do with your clothes?" said the groceryman, as he snuffed around, as though he thought he could smell something.

"O, we bought new clothes in New Orleans, and let our old ones out of the window of a hotel with a rope. A man picked them up, and they sent him to the quarantine for smallpox patients. O, we came out all right, but it was a close call. Say, I bet this prairie dog can lick your cat in a holy minute," and the boy pushed the dog against the cat, said "sik em," and the cat scratched the dog, the dog yelled and bit the cat, the cat run up the shelves, over the canned goods, and tipped over some bottles of pickles, and the old groceryman got crazy, while the boy took his prairie dog under his arm, and his horned toad in his hand and started to go out.

"I'll drop in some day and have some fun with you," says the boy.

"If you do I will stab you with a cheese knife," said the groceryman as he picked up the broken glass.

CHAPTER XV.

The Bad Boy's Joke with a Stuffed Rattlesnake — He Tells the Old Groceryman About his Dad's Morbid Appetite.

The old groceryman was sitting on the counter, with his legs stretched lengthwise, his heels resting on a sack of flour, and his back against a pile of wrapping paper, his eyes closed, his pipe gone out, and the ashes sifting from it on the cat that was asleep in his lap. He was waiting for a customer to come in and buy something to start the day's business. He had sprinkled the floor and swept the dirt up in a corner, and he was sleepy. There was a crash in front of the door, a barrel of axe handles and garden tools had been tipped over on the sidewalk, the door opened with a jerk and closed with a slam, and the bad boy came in with a long paper bax, perforated with holes, slammed it on the counter beside the groceryman's legs, and yelled:

"Wake up, Rip Van Winkle, the day of judgment has come, and you are still buried. You get a move on you or the procession will go off and leave you. Say, are you afraid of rattlesnakes?" and the bad boy shook the paper box, when an enormous rattle came from within, as though a snake had shaken its tail good and plenty.

"Great Scott, boy, I believe you have got a rattlesnake in that box," and he jumped off the counter and grabbed an iron fire poker, while the boy got out his knife to cut the string on the box. "Now, look here, I am suffering from nervous prostration, and a snake turned loose in this store would settle it with me. I am at your mercy, but by the holy smoke, if I am bitten by that snake I will kill you and your old snake. Now take that box out of here," and the old man picked up a hatchet and got behind a barrel.

"Well, wouldn't that skin you," said the bad boy, as he sharpened his knife on a piece of old cheese, and felt of the edge. "Here you have been telling me for years what a brave man you were, and how you were not afraid of anything that wore hair, and now you have fits because a little five-foot rattlesnake, with only ten rattles on, makes a formal call on you. Gee, but you are a squaw. Why, there is no danger in the bite of a rattlesnake, since science has taken the matter up. All you got to do, when a snake bites you and you begin to turn black, is to drink a couple of quarts of whisky, and bind a poultice of limberg cheese on the wound, and go to bed for a week or ten days, and you come out all right," and the bad boy began to cut the string.

"Now, let up until I wait on these customers," said the old man, as he went to the door and let in a committee of women who were to buy some supplies for a church sociable. The women lined up on each side of the store, looking at the canned things on the shelves, and the old man was trying to be polite, when the bad boy opened the box and laid on the floor a stuffed rattlesnake that was as natural as life, and touched a rattle box in his pocket, and the trouble began. The women saw the snake curled up, ready to spring, and they all went through the door at once, tipping over everything that was loose, and screaming, while the old man, when he saw the snake, got into the front show window and trembled and yelled for the police. A policeman rushed in the store and when he saw the snake he backed out of the door, and the bad boy sat down on a box and began to eat some raisins out of a box, as though he was not particularly interested in the commotion.

"Arrest that boy with the snake," said the groceryman.

"Come out of that wid your menagerie," said the policeman, shaking his club.

"Come in and get the snake if you want it," said the boy, "I don't want it any more, anyway," and he took the stuffed snake up by the head and laid it across his lap, and began to shake the rattles, and laugh at the groceryman and the policeman, and the crowd that had collected in front of the store. The policeman came in laughing, and the old groceryman crawled out of the show window, and all breathed free again, and finally the policeman went and drove the crowd away, and went on his beat again, after shaking his club at the boy; the groceryman, the snake and the cat remained in the store. The groceryman took a swig out of a bottle of whisky, to settle his nerves, and the took up his snake and pushed it towards the cat, which ran up a stepladder and yowled.

"Do you know, I kind of like you," said the old groceryman, as he went up behind the bad boy and took him by the throat, "and I think it would be a great thing for the community if I should just choke you to death. You are worse than a mad dog, and you are just ruining my business."

"I will give you just ten seconds to take you hand off my neck," said the bad boy, pulling out a dollar watch, "and when the time is up, and you have not let loose of me, I will turn loose a couple of live snakes I have in my pocket, and some tarantulas, and you will probably be bitten and swell up like a poisoned pup, and die under the counter."

"All right, let's be friends," said the old man, as he let go of the bad boy. "If your parents and the rest of the community can stand having you around, alive, probably it is my duty to be a martyr, and stand my share, but you are very trying to the nerves. By the way, put that confounded stuffed snake in the ice box, and sit down here and tell me something. I saw your father on the street yesterday, and he is a sight. His stomach is twice as big around as it was, and he looks troubled. What has got into him?"

"Well, I'll tell you, dad has got what they call a morbid appetite. Whatever you do, old skate, don't you ever get a morbid appetite."

"What is a morbid appetite?" asked the old man; as he peeled a banana and began to eat it. "I can always eat anything that is not tied down, but I don't know about this morbid business."

"Scientists say a morbid appetite is one that don't know when it has got enough. Dad likes good things, but he wants all there is on the table. Now, at New Orleans, before we came home, dad and I went in a restaurant to get some oysters, and you know the oysters there are the biggest in the world. When we got there dad was hungry, and the thought of raw oysters on the half shell made him morbid. He had a blue point appetite, and ordered four dozen on the half shell, for himself, and one dozen for me. Well, you would have dropped dead in your tracks if you had been there. Six waiters brought on the five dozen oysters, and each oyster was as big as a pie plate. Six dozen oysters would cover this floor from the door to the ice box. Dad almost fainted when he saw them, but his pride was at stake, and he made up his mind if he didn't eat them all the waiters would think he was a tenderfoot, and so he started in. The first oyster was as big as a calf's liver, and nobody but a sword swallower could ever have got it down. Dad cut one oyster into quarters, and got away with it, and after a while he murdered another, and after he had eaten three he wanted to go home and leave them. Then is the time his little boy got in his work. I told dad that if he didn't eat all the oysters the waiters and the people would mob him, that it was a deadly offense to order oysters and not eat them, and that they would probably kill us both before we got out of the place. He said, 'Hennery, I don't like oysters like I used to, and it seems to me I couldn't eat another one to save my life, but if, as you say, we are in a country where a man's life is held so cheaply, by the great horn spoons, I will eat every oyster in the house, and the Lord have mercy on me.' I told him that was about the size of it, and he would eat or die, and maybe he would die anyway, and just then a wicked-looking negro with a big oyster knife came to the table and looked ugly at dad and said, 'Have another dozen?' and dad said, 'Yes,' and then he began to eat as though his life depended on it, and I could hear the great wads of oysters strike with a dull thud on exposed places inside of dad, and before he got up from the table he had eaten them all, and he told the man we would be in again to lunch after awhile. Dad is the bravest man I ever saw, and don't you forget it. He would have come out all right, I suppose, and lived, if it hadn't been for his devilish morbid appetite for travel and adventure. Quick as we got out of the oyster place dad wanted to take a steamboat ride down the river to the Eades Jetties at the mouth of the river, and we went on board, and had a nice ride down to the mouth. After we had looked over the jetties where Eades made an artificial canal big enough for the largest ocean steamers to come up to New Orleans, the passengers wanted the captain to run the boat outside the bar, into the blue ocean, where the waves come from. Gee, but I hope I may live long enough to forget the ride. We hadn't got a boat's length outside the bar before the boat began to roll and toss, and I held on to dad's hand, and wished I was dead. I told him my little tummy ached, and I wanted a lemon. Dad said

my little tummy, with its three oysters in it, was not worth men-
tioning, and told me to look at him. Talk about your Mount Pelee,
and your Vesuvius, those volcanoes were tame and uninteresting,
compared to dad, leaning over the railing, and shouting words at
the sharks in the water. Why? he just doubled up like a jack knife,
one minute, and then straightened up like an elephant standing on
its hind legs in a circus, the next minute, and he kept saying, 'Ye-
up,' and all the passengers said 'poor man.' I told them he was not
so poor, for he owned a brewery at home. Dad finally went to sleep
with his arm and head over the rail, and his body hanging limp,
down on deck. The boat turned around and went back into the
mouth of the river, and the passengers were thanking the captain
for giving them such a lovely ride, when I thought I would wake
dad up, and so I touched him on the shoulder and asked him if he
didn't want a few dozen more raw oysters, and he yelled murder,
and began to have hydrophobia again, and bump himself. You
know the way people do when they are dissatisfied with the medicine the doctor gives. Well, we got back to New Orleans, and dad
took a hack to the hotel, and told the driver not to pass any saloon
where there were oyster shells on the sidewalk. We came home
next day. Well, I guess I will get my snake out of the ice box, and go
home and comfort dad. But wait a minute till that Irishman puts
that chunk of ice in the ice box, and see if he notices the snake."
Just then there was a sound as if a house had fallen, a two hundred
pound cake of ice struck the floor, and the Irishman came running
through the grocery with his ice tongs waving, and yelling,
"There's a rattlesnake in yer ice box, mister, and ye can go to h — l
for yer ice." The groceryman looked at the boy, and the boy looked
at the groceryman, the cat looked at both, the boy took his snake
under his arm and went out, and the old man said:

"Well, you are the limit. Call again, and bring an anaconda,
and a man-eating tiger," and he went and scraped up the ice.

CHAPTER XVI.

The Bad Boy Tells the Story of the Bears in Yellowstone Park and How Brave Dad Was.

The old groceryman was down on his knees, with a wet cloth, swabbing up something from the floor with one hand, while he held his nose with the other, his back toward the door, when suddenly the door opened with a bank, striking the old man in the back, knocking him over and landing him with his head in a basket of strictly fresh eggs, breaking at least a dozen of them, and filling the air with an odor that was unmistakable; and the bad boy followed the door into the grocery.

"What's your notion of taking a nap, with a basket of stale eggs for a pillow," said the bad boy, as he took the old man by the arm and raised him up, and looked at him with a grin that was tantalizing. "What is it, sewer gas? My, but the board of health won't do a thing to you if the inspector happens in here. Those eggs must have been mislaid by a hen that had a diseased mind," and the bad boy took a bottle of cologne out of the show case and began to sprinkle the floor, and squirted some of it on the old man's clothes.

"Say, do you know I bought those eggs of a man dressed like a farmer, who came in here yesterday with his pants in his boots, and smelling as though he had just come out of his cow stable?" said the old groceryman, as he took a piece of coffee sack and wiped yellow egg off his whiskers. "And yet they are old enough to attend caucuses. I tell you that you have got to watch a farmer the same as you do a crook, or he will get the best of you. And to think I sold four dozen of those eggs to a church sociable committee that is going to make ice cream for a celebration tonight. But what in thunder do you come in here for, like a toboggin, and knock me all over the floor, into eggs, when you could come in gently and save a fellow's life; and me a sick man, too. Ever since that explosion, when we tried to see how they blow up battleships, I have had nervous prostration, and I am just about sick of this condemned foolishness. I like to keep posted on current events, and want to learn how things are going on outside in the world, and I realize that for an old man to associate with a bright boy like you keeps him young, but, by ginger, when I think how you have done me up several times, I sometimes think I better pick out a boy that is not so strenuous, so you can tell your Pa I rather he wouldn't trade here any more, for him to keep you away from here. It is hard on me, I know, but life is dear to all of us, and the life insurance company that I am contributing to has notified me that if I don't quit having you around they will cancel my policy. Now, you may say farewell, and get out of here forever, and I will try and pull along with the cat, and such boys as come in here to be sociable. Go on now," and the old groceryman threw the eggs out in the alley, and washed his whiskers at the sink.

"Oh, I guess not," said the boy, as he sat down on a tin cracker box and began to eat figs out of a box. "I know something about the law myself, and if you drive me away, you could be arrested for breach of promise, and arson, and you would go to the penitentiary. It was all I could do to make the police believe you didn't set this old shebang afire to get the insurance, and my being here has drawn more custom to your store than the quality of your goods would warrant. No, sir, I stay right here, and advise with you, and keep you out of trouble. If I went home and told dad what you said he would fall in a fit, and would sue you for damages for ruining my reputation, if he didn't come over here with a club and take it out of your hide. Dad can stand a good many things, but when anybody insults one of our family, dad gets violent, and he had rather kill a man than eat. You read about their finding the body of a man in an alley, with his head crushed? Well, I don't want to say anything, but it is rumored that dad was seen near that alley the night before, and that man chased me once for throwing snow balls at him. We move in good society, and are looked upon as good citizens, but dad's temper gets worse every year. Can I stay around here more or less, or do I have to go out into the world, branded as a criminal, because an old fool fell into a basket of his own eggs? Say, now, answer up quick," and the bad boy sharpened a match with a big dirk knife and picked fig seeds out of his teeth.

"Oh, sugar, no; you don't need to go," said the old groceryman, as he came up to the boy, wiping the soapsuds off, and trying to smile. "I was only joshing you, and, honestly, I enjoy you. Life is a dreary burden when you are away. Somehow I have got so my blood gets thick, and my appetite fails, when you are away from town, and when you play some low down trick on me, while I seem mad at the time, it does me good, starts the circulation, and when you go away I seem a new man, and laugh, and feel like I had been off on a vacation, fishing, or something. It was a great mistake that I did not have a family of boys to keep me mad part of the time, because a man that never has anything to make him mad is no good. I envy your dad in having you around constantly to keep his blood in circulation. I suppose you are responsible for his being, at his age, as spry as a boy. He told me when he and you got back from Yellowstone park last summer that the trip did him a world of good, and that he got so he could climb a tree — just shin right up like a cat, and that you were the bravest boy he ever saw, said that you would fight a bear as quick as eat. Such a boy I am proud to call my friend. What was it about your fighting bears, single-handed, with no weapon but empty tomato cans? You ought to be in the history books. Your dad said bravery run in the family."

"Oh, get out. Did dad tell you about that bear story?" said the bad boy, as he sharpened his knife on his boot. "Well, you'd a dide right there, if you could have seen dad.

He is one of these men that is brave sort of intermittent, like folks have fever. Half the time he is a darn coward, but when you don't expect it, for instance when the pancakes are burned, or the steak is raw, and his dyspepsia seems to work just right, he will flare up and sass the cook, and I don't know of anything braver than that; but ordinarily he is meek as a lam. I think the stomach has a good deal to do with a man's bravery. You take a soldier in battle, and if he is hungry he is full of fight, but you fill him up with baked beans and things and he is willing to postpone a fight, and he don't care whether there is any fight at all or not. I think the trip through Yellowstone park took the tar out of dad. Those geysers throwing up hot water, apparently right out of the hot place the preachers tell about, seemed to set him to thinking that may be he had got nearer h — l, on a railroad pass, than he had ever expected to get. He told me, one day, when we stood beside old Faithful geyser, and the hot water belched up into the air a hundred feet, that all it wanted was for the lid to be taken off, and h — l would be yawning right there, and he was going to try to lead a different life, and if he ever got out of that park alive he should go home and join every church in town, and he should advise ministers to get the sinners to take a trip to the park, if they wanted to work religion into them. Dad would wake up in the night, at the hotels in the park, when a geyser went off suddenly, and groan, and cross himself, as he had seen religious people do, and tell me that in a few days more we would be safe out of the d — n place, and you would never catch him in it again.

"Well, there is one hotel where a lot of bears come out of the woods in the evening, to eat the garbage that is thrown out from the hotel. They are wild bears, all right, but they have got so tame that they come right near folks, and don't do anything but eat garbage and growl, and fight each other. The cook told me about it, and said there was no danger, 'cause you could take a club and scare them into the woods.

"We got to the hotel in the afternoon, and dad went to our room to say his prayers, and take a nap, and had his supper taken to the room, and he was so scared at the awful surroundings in the park that he asked a blessing on the supper, though it was the bummest supper I ever struck. After dark I told dad we better go out and take a walk and inspect the scenery, 'cause it was all in the bill, and if you got a bum supper and didn't get the scenery you were losing money on the deal. I saw the man emptying the garbage and I knew the bears would be getting in their work pretty soon, so I took dad and we walked away off, and he talked about how God had prepared that park as a warning to sinners of what was to come, and I knew his system was sort of running down, and I knew he needed excitement, a shock or something to make a reaction, so I steered him around by the garbage pile.

"Say, before he knew it we were right in the midst of about nine bears, grizzlies, cinnamon bears, black bears, and all of them raised up and said, 'Whoof!' and they growled, and, by gosh, just as quick as I could run this knife into your liver, I missed dad. He just yelled: 'Hennery, this is the limit, and here is where your poor old dad sprints for tall timber,' and he made for a tree, and I yelled: 'Hurry up, dad!' and he said: 'I ain't walking, am I?' and you ought to have seen his short legs carry him to the tree, and help him skin up it. I have seen squirrels climb trees, when a dog was after them, but they were slow compared to dad. When he got up to a limb he yelled to me to come on up, as he wanted to give me a few last instructions about settling his estate, but I told him I was going to play I was Daniel in the lion's den, so I studied the bears for a while and let dad yell for the police, and then I picked up an armful of tomato cans and made a rush for the bears, and yelled and threw cans at them, and pretty soon every bear went off into the woods, growling and scrapping with each other, and I told dad to come down and I would save him at the risk of my life. Dad came down as quick as he went up, and I took his arm and led him to the hotel, and when we got to the room he would have collapsed, only I gave him a big drink of whiskey, and then he braced up and said: 'Hennery, when it comes to big game, you and I are the wonders of the world. You are brave, and I am discreet, and we make a team hard to beat.' I told dad he covered himself with glory, but that he left most of his pants on the tree, but he said he didn't care for a few pants when he had a boy that was the bravest that ever came down the pike. When we got home alive he didn't join the church, but he gave me a gold watch. Well, I'll have to depart," and the bad boy went out and left the old groceryman thinking of the hereafter.

CHAPTER XVII.

The Bad Boy and the Groceryman Illustrate the Russia-Japanese War — The Bad Boy Tells About Dad's Efforts to Raise Hair by the "Sunshine" Method.

The old groceryman had a war map spread out on the counter, and for an hour he had stood up in front of it, reading a morning paper, with his thumb on Port Arthur, his fingers covering the positions occupied by the Japanese and Russian forces in Manchuria, and his face working worse than the face of the Czar eating a caviar sandwich and ordering troops to the far east, at the same time shying at dynamite bombs of nihilists. There was a crash in front of the grocery and the old man jumped behind a barrel, thinking Port Arthur had been blown up, and the Russian fleet torpedoed.

"Hello, Matsuma, you young monkey," said the old man, as the bad boy burst the door open and rushed in with a shovel at shoulder arms, and came to "present arms" in front of the old man, who came from behind the barrel and acknowledged the salute. "Say, now honest did you put that chunk of ice in the stove the day you skipped out last?"

"Sure Mike!" said the boy, as he ran the shovel under the cat that was sleeping by the stove, and tossed her into a barrel of dried apples. "I wanted to demonstrate to you, old Michaelovitski, the condition of things at Vladivostok, where you candle-eating Russians are bottled up in the ice, and where we Japanese are going to make you put on your skates and get away to Siberia. What are you doing with the map of the seat of war?"

"Oh, I was only trying to figure out the plan of campaign, and find out where the Japanese would go to when they are licked," said the old man. "This thing is worrying me. I want to see Russia win, and I think our government ought to send to them all the embalmed beef we had left from the war with Spain, but if we did you monkey Japanese would capture it, and have a military funeral over it, and go on eating fish and rice. When this country was in trouble, in 1864, the Russians sent a fleet of warships to New York and notified all Europe to stand back and look pleasant, and by the great horn spoons, I am going to stand by Russia or bust. I would like to be over there at Port Arthur and witness an explosion of a torpedo under something. Egad, but I glory in the smell of gunpowder. Now, say, here is Port Arthur, by this barrel of dried apples, and there is Mushapata, by the ax handle barrel, see?"

"Well, you and I are just alike," said the boy. "Let's have a sham battle, right here in the grocery. Get down that can of powder."

"'Taint against the law, is it?" said the old man as he handed down a tin cannister of powder. "I want excitement, and valuable information, but I don't want to unduly excite the neighbors."

"Oh, don't worry about the neighbors," said the boy, as he poured a little powder under the barrel of dried apples. "Now, as you say, this is Port Arthur. This chest of Oolong tea represents a Japanese cruiser outside the harbor. This box of codfish represents a Russian fort, see? and the stove represents a Russian cruiser. This barrel of ax handles is the Russian army, entrenched behind the bag of coffee. Now, we put a little powder under all of thems and lay a train from one to the other, and now you get out a few of those giant firecrackers you had left over from last Fourth of July, and a Roman candle, and we can illustrate the whole business so Alexovitch and Ito would take to the woods."

"No danger, is there?" said the old groceryman, as he brought out the fireworks, looking as happy and interested as the bad boy did. "I want to post myself on war in the far east, but I don't want to do anything that would occasion remark."

"Oh, remark nothing," said the boy, as he fixed a firecracker under a barrel of rice, another under a tin can of soda crackers, and got the Roman candle ready to touch off at the stove. "It will not make any more fuss than faking a flash-light photograph. Just a piff — s — s — sis — boom — and there you are, full of information."

"Well, let-er-go-Galiagher," said the old man, sort of reckless like, as he got behind the cheese box. "Gol darn the expense, when you want to illustrate your ideas of war."

The boy lit the Roman candle, got behind a barrel of potatoes and turned the spluttering Roman candle on the giant firecracker under the stove, and when he saw the fuse of the firecracker was lighted, he turned the torch on the powder under the barrel of dried apples, and in a second everything went kiting; the barrel of dried apples with the cat in it went up to the ceiling, the stove was blown over the counter, the cheese box and the old groceryman went with a crash to the back end of the store, the front windows blew out on the sidewalk, the store was full of smoke, the old man rushed out the back door with his whiskers singed and yelled "Fire!" while the bad boy fell out the front door his eye winkers gone, and his hair singed, the cat got out with no hair to brag on, and before they could breathe twice the fire department came clattering up to a hydrant and soon turned the hose inside the grocery. There was not very much fire, and after tipping over every barrel and box that had not been blown skyhigh the firemen gave one last look at the inside of the grocery, one last squirt at the burned and singed cat, that had crawled into a bag of cinnamon on the top shelf, and they went away, leaving the doors and windows open; the crowd dispersed, and the bad boy went in the front door; peered around under the counter, pulled the cork out of a bottle of olive oil and began to anoint himself where he had been scorched. Hearing a shuffling of arctic overshoes filled with water, in the back shed, and a still small voice, saying, "Well, I'll be condemned," he looked up and saw the red face of the old groceryman peeking in the back door.

"Come in, Alexandroviski, and rub some of this sweet oil on your countenance, and put some kerosene on your head, where the hair was. Gee! but you are a sight! Don't you go out anywhere and let a horse see you, or he will run away."

"Have all the forts and warships come down yet?" said the old man, looking up toward the ceiling, holding up his elbow to ward off any possible descending barrel or stove lid. "I now realize the truth of General Sherman's remark that war is hell. Gosh! how it smarts where the skin is burnt off.

"Give me some of that salad oil," and the old man sopped the oil on his face and head, and the boy rubbed his lips and ears, and they looked at each other and tried to smile, two cracked, and wrinkled and scorched smiles, across the counter at each other. "Now, you little Japanese monkey, I hope you are satisfied, after you have wrecked my store, and fitted me for the hospital, and I want you to get out of here, and never come back. By ginger, I know when I have got enough war. They can settle that affair at Mukden, or Holoyahoo, or any old place. I wash my hands of the whole business. Git, you Spitz. What did you pour so much powder around the floor for? All I wanted was a little innocent illustration of the horrors of war, not an explosion."

"Th — at's what I wanted, too," said the boy, as he looked up on the top shelf at the cat, that was licking herself where the hair used to be. "How did I know that powder would burn so quick? Say, you are unreasonable. Do you think I will go off and leave you to die here under the counter of bloodpoisoning, like a dog that has eaten a loaded sausage? Never! I am going to nurse you through this thing, and bring you out as good as new. I know how you feel towards me. Dad felt the same way towards me, down in Florida, the time he got skun. You old people don't seem to appreciate a boy that tries to teach you useful nollig."

"What about your dad getting skun in Florida? I never heard about it," said the old groceryman, as he took a hand mirror and looked at his burned face.

"Why, that was when we first got down there," said the boy, looking at the old man and laughing. "Gee! but you would make a boy laugh if his lips were chapped. You look like a greased pig at a barbecue. Well, when we struck Florida, and dad got so he could assimilate high balls, and eat oranges off the trees, like a giraf, he said he wanted to go fishing, and get tanned up, so we hired a boat and I rowed while dad fished, I ask him why he didn't try that new prescription to raise hair on his bald head that I read of in a magazine, to go bareheaded in the sun. He ask me if anybody ever raised any hair on a bald head that way, and I told him about Mr, Rockefeller, who had only one hair on his head, and he played golf bareheaded and in two weeks had to have his hair cut with a lawn mower, 'cause it made his brain ache. Dad said if Rockefeller could raise hair by the sunshine method he could, and he threw his straw hat overboard, and began to fish in the sun for fish and hair. Well, you'd a dide to see dad's head after the blisters began to raise. First, he thought the blisters was hair, but when we got back to the hotel and he looked in a glass, he see it wasn't hair worth a cent. His head and face looked like one of these hippopotamuses, and dad was mad. If I could have got dad in a side show I could have made a barrel of money, but he won't never make a show of his self, not even to make money, he is so proud. There is more proud flesh on dad than there is on any man I ever nursed. Well, dad ask me what was good for blisters, and I told him lime juice was the best thing, so he sent me to get some limes. They are a little sour thing, like a lemon, and I told him to cut one in two and soak the juice on his head and face, and I went to supper, 'cause dad looked so disreputable he wouldn't go to the dining room. When I bought the limes the man gave me a green persimmon, and of course dad got the persimmon instead of the lime, and when I came back to our room after supper dad was in bed, yelling for a doctor. Say, you know how a persimmon puckers your mouth up when you eat it? Well, dad had just sopped himself with persimmon juice, and his head was puckered up like the hide of an elephant, and his face and cheeks were drawn around sideways, and wrinkled so I was scart. I gave him a mirror to look at his self, and when he got one look he said: 'Hennery, it is all over with your dad, you might just as well call in a lawyer to take my measure for a will, and an undertaker to fill me with stuff so I will keep till they get me home by express, with handles on. What was that you called that fruit I sopped my head with?' and he groaned like he was at a revival. Well, I told him he had used the persimmon instead of the lime juice I told him to, and that I would cure him, so I got a cake of dog soap and laundered dad, and put on stuff to take the swelling out, and the next day he began to notice things, it would have been all right only a chambermaid told somebody the mean old man with the pretty boy in 471 had the smallpox, and that settled it. You know in a hotel they are offal sensitive about smallpox, 'cause all the boarders will leave if a man has a pimple on his self, so they made dad and I go into quarantine in a hen house for a week, and dad said it was all my fault trying to get him to raise hair like Rockefeller. Well, I must go home and explain to ma how I lost my hair and eye-winkers. If I was in your place I would take a little tar and put it on where your hair was before the explosion," and the bad boy went out, leaving the old groceryman drawing some tar out of the barrel, on to a piece of brown paper, and dabbling it on his head with his finger.

THE END